e had done the marriage thing and failed
rably. The idea of trying something light and
ings with Makena might work if she weren't
st friend's baby sister and a woman he
would expect more than a few nights of
ingless sex.

deserved more—deserved better than him.

orked long hours and traveled all the time. He
d his job with the Corcoran Team, the off-the-
s undercover group that took on high-risk
ue jobs for companies and governments. He
with danger. Thrived on it.

TAMED

—

HELENKAY DIMON

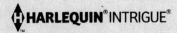

HARLEQUIN® INTRIGUE®

To Allison Lyons for her patience, support and editing.
I appreciate everything you do
even though I sometimes forget to say it.

ISBN-13: 978-0-373-74906-5

Tamed

Copyright © 2015 by HelenKay Dimon

Recycling programs
for this product may
not exist in your area.

Printed in U.S.A.

HelenKay Dimon, an award-winning author, spent twelve years in the most unromantic career ever—divorce lawyer. After dedicating all that effort to helping people terminate relationships, she is thrilled to deal in happy endings and write romance novels for a living. Now her days are filled with gardening, writing, reading and spending time with her family in and around San Diego. Stop by her website, helenkaydimon.com, and say hello.

Books by HelenKay Dimon

Harlequin Intrigue

Corcoran Team: Bulletproof Bachelors

Cornered
Sheltered
Tamed

Corcoran Team

Fearless
Ruthless
Relentless
Lawless
Traceless

Mystery Men

Under the Gun
Guns and the Girl Next Door
Gunning for Trouble
Locked and Loaded
The Big Guns

Visit the Author Profile page at Harlequin.com for more titles.

CAST OF CHARACTERS

Shane Baker—The lone bachelor on the Corcoran Team. He's been traveling for work and running away from his feelings for his best friend's little sister. A bad marriage and very real sense he's not the marrying kind make him the right guy to stay on the move, but his feelings for Makena test him...and he's not going anywhere until he finds out who's after her.

Makena Kingston—Makena spent a lifetime searching for a purpose. She's not tough and lethal like her big brother, but she can contribute. Working behind the scenes, researching the men who lie about being war heroes, gives her that direction. The job also helps her forget Shane, the man she's always loved...and the person who's there for her when gunmen come hunting.

Jeff Horvath—A guy with an excellent shot and wilderness training. He once claimed to be someone else and having his lie uncovered fuels his fury. He doesn't hide his hatred for Makena and keeps showing up in all the wrong places. The only way to save Makena may be to unmask him one more time.

Tyler Cowls—The owner of the Wall of Dishonor website. He spends his days exposing men who lie about their military service. The work is anonymous, but the site angers a lot of people. Has he accidentally put Makena in danger...or is something else going on?

Frank Jay—He made a mistake and got caught in a lie. He claims he wants to make amends but it's hard to trust a man who once claimed to be a SEAL and lost everything when the truth came out.

Cameron Roth—Shane's fellow team member. Cam survived falling in love while on assignment. Watching Shane struggle, Cam wonders if his friend will be able to balance his feelings for Makena and his responsibilities on the job.

and general lack of updating helped her afford the place.

Maybe fifteen feet separated her deck from the one next door. Sometimes she could hear her neighbors, a young married couple, argue. They did that a lot, and about everything. Makena often thought marital longevity might not be on their side.

The night fell over Lannaker Estates, the fancy name for the development of cozy single-level homes perched on a small hill overlooking the Chester River. This part of Maryland, the Eastern Shore, possessed the bucolic feel of a university town, which it was. Small and quaint, close to the Chesapeake Bay and about an hour and a half from Washington, DC. Nothing much happened in Chestertown, and she liked it that way.

For the five hundred and first time, she glanced out back on her Shane watch. This time she saw a dark SUV parked parallel to the neighbor couple's back porch. She couldn't make out the exact color thanks to the fading early fall sunlight. Probably just someone coming to referee the fighting couple's newest argument.

She could make out two people...wearing all black. That struck her as a little much for this time of year. They'd moved out of shorts weather, but the cool breezes hadn't started yet.

Yeah, all black and...she balanced her palms

on the counter and leaned in closer. She blinked a few times as she tried to figure out what she was seeing. It was as if the two people—men, she thought from their wide-shouldered builds— stalked the house. They separated. One stopped at a utility box attached to the house and did something. She couldn't quite tell what. The other went to the back door and dropped down on one knee.

Then they raced. Stormed the back of the neighbor's house. She switched from the window at the sink to the one on the side of her house. With her back to the wall, she peeked around the window frame and watched a bulky figure run through the back of the house next door.

Her heartbeat thundered in her ears, and her chest ached from the force of her heavy breathing. When a bang rang out in the quiet night, she gasped. She fought to drag air into her lungs, but her body stopped working. As if the messages from her brain just kept misfiring.

She stood, frozen, as her gaze searched from window to window, looking for any sign of movement. Thoughts jumbled in her muddled brain and she tried to think. It was as if someone had thrown a blanket over her, slowing down every movement and blocking every thought. She needed to do something. She should…the phone.

She patted her back pockets but couldn't feel

her cell. She didn't have a landline, so she depended on the cell. Fear clogged her throat and a frantic desperation made her movements jerky. She glanced around and forced her brain to reboot. The family room. That was where she'd left it, so if she could get there she could call out.

A weird sensation washed over her. Her head whipped around and she saw him. A looming figure standing in the window directly across from her. He had the edge of the curtains in his fist. Even with the mask she could feel his furious glare.

Then he was gone.

She took off at a dash. Crossed the threshold and stopped at the fireplace. She threw the stack of magazines on the floor and ran around the coffee table. Laptop. Remote control. No cell.

She heard knocking in her head. A deafening series of thuds. It took her a few seconds to figure out the noise came from outside the cottage, not inside her mind. The back door crashed in. Wood splintered and the glass of the small window at the top of the door cracked.

Footsteps echoed around her. She could barely make out any sound over the clipped panting escaping her throat. She turned around and slammed her knee into the table but kept moving. Standing still meant death. Holt and Shane had drummed that into her head. Fight back. Scream.

She started to do just that.

"Help!" Her voice cut off when the attacker slammed into her.

She felt the force as if she'd run at high speed into a steel wall. Her teeth rattled and her head snapped back. The breath left her body. No mattered how she fought for balance, her feet slid across the floor.

Arms wrapped around her waist in a crushing band. The room spun as she fell back. She waited for the punishing thump against the floor, but it never came. Her butt bounced against the couch cushion just as the attacker's body came toward her.

Tension choked the room. She went from thinking and feeling to autopilot. Before the attacker could use his weight to press her down, she scrambled. Pivoted to the left and kept going. She reached out to stop her fall, but it was too late. She kept going until she landed with a jolt on her hands and knees.

Something crunched under her leg. She grabbed it as she tried to run. She got maybe a foot before a hand latched on to her calf. A tight hand squeezed her muscle until she cried out in pain.

The aches mixed with the fear as her heartbeat kicked up even higher. She felt the burning in her palm and looked down. She didn't know when she'd found her cell, but she held it.

She kicked out against the grip on her leg. Looked around for something to throw. Tried to keep her mind engaged as terror took off inside her.

The attacker regained his balance and climbed to his feet, never letting go of her leg. She hopped as she tried to make the call. Her eyes focused long enough for her to see the terrifying message: no signal.

She was on her own.

Dizziness hit her out of nowhere. He yanked on her leg and sent her sprawling backward. This time she missed the couch. The free fall ended with a hard smack against the hardwood floor. Her elbow made contact first and her hand went numb. The useless cell dropped and bounced.

She tried to turn over and he fell on top of her. His legs straddled her sides and his hand tightened on her throat. Seemingly using almost none of his strength, he flipped her over onto her back. Dead black eyes stared down at her.

"Move and you die." He slipped a knife out and flashed it in front of her eyes. "Do not test me."

"I don't have anything." She tried to shake her head, but he kept her locked against the floor. "I work at the university. I don't—"

He tightened his hand. "Shut up."

Survival instinct kicked in. She grabbed for

the hand, trying to pry his fingers away as he choked off her breath. Desperate to gain traction, she shifted her hips. Her feet slipped across the floor.

Fear clamped down on her. The adrenaline pumping through her gave her a burst of energy. She slapped against him, against the floor. Her gaze whipped around the room as she looked for something to make into a weapon. Anything.

"It's over." The ominous threat sounded even worse in the attacker's flat tone.

"No." She said the word as much to herself as to him.

She had to stay conscious and clear even as panic bombarded her. It became harder and harder to breathe. He outweighed her. His strength far surpassed hers. Which meant she had to depend on her smarts.

But she was running out of options and air. As her vision darkened around the edges, she remembered the fireplace and the poker. While she wrestled with the hand crushing her windpipe, she shimmied. Moved on her back as he shifted and increased his grip.

With one last surge of energy, she threw her arm out to the side. The move nearly wrenched it out of the socket, but when she didn't touch anything she did it again. This time she knocked over the small vase holding the fireplace tools.

The poker hit the back of her hand and rolled. The handle slipped away from her fingers, but she lunged and caught it. Cool metal filled her palm.

She tightened her grip and prepared to swing.

SHANE BAKER ARRIVED in Chestertown an hour before Makena's suggested dinnertime. He broke a few traffic laws getting to her, speeding being one of them. But instead of going in right away, he parked at the opposite end of her cottage complex and walked along the river, trying to clear his head.

Makena was off-limits. He'd done the marriage thing once and failed miserably. The idea of trying something light and no strings with Makena might work if she weren't his best friend's baby sister and a woman he knew would expect more than a few nights of meaningless sex. She deserved more. Deserved better than him.

He worked long hours and traveled all the time. He loved his job with the Corcoran Team, the off-the-books undercover group that took on high-risk rescue jobs for companies and governments. He lived with danger. Thrived on it.

Dragging Makena into that life, no matter how hard it was to forget her face even as he traveled thousands of miles away, would be a mistake.

Dinner wasn't even a good idea, but he couldn't say no. Holt was out of town, enjoying some time off with Lindsey, his new girlfriend. Shane rationalized his presence at Makena's back door as he walked toward it. He needed to watch over her. No kissing. No fun. Just two old friends talking.

Now if he could only get his brain and body on the same page.

He rounded the far corner of the complex. Heard the crunch of wood just as he saw Makena's back door implode. Before his mind could process, he took off. He ran along the edge of the hill and sprinted to the porch. Up and inside just as he heard her scream, then voices.

His heart hammered in his chest as he silently hoped he wasn't too late. He shot through the doorway. A series of grunts and thuds greeted him as he glanced around the small space. His eyes finally focused. It took him until then to realize the lights had blinked out. But he had no time to worry about that now. He had to get to her.

With his gun out, he approached in rapid speed. He was about to call out when something flashed through the air. She had something in her hand and swung it in an arc. It connected with the attacker's shoulder.

The guy let out a roar. His big body shud-

dered, but he didn't fall. Shane took care of
that part. He switched his grip on the gun and
whacked the guy in the side of the head with all
his strength. The attacker dropped in a crumpled heap.

Then Shane focused on Makena. Her eyes
wide and glassy. A ripped shirt and her long
black hair half-pulled out of her ponytail. He'd
never been happier to see her.

He took a step forward and she scooted back
on her butt as if fear still held her in its grasp.
"Makena, are you okay?"

Some of the haze cleared. She blinked and her
shoulders fell. "Shane?"

"Come here, baby." He stepped over the unmoving body to get to her.

In one lift he had her up and in his arms. His
hands shook with relief, but that was nothing
compared to the trembling moving through her.
Much harder and she'd break apart. His palm
smoothed over her hair as he scanned the room.
He had no idea what was going on, but the guy
on the floor wasn't exactly dressed for a social
visit.

Once he had them out of the immediate grabbing area if the guy should wake up, Shane
pulled back from her. As gently as possible, he
lifted her head to look into her eyes. "Did he
hurt you?"

"There were two of them." Her voice sounded small and shaky, totally unlike her usual spunky go-get-'em attitude.

The news sent a shot of adrenaline coursing through him. He slipped her behind him and faced the open area. The squeal of tires echoed in the distance. Shane left her only long enough to run to the back door. He caught sight of the back of a dark SUV. No license plate.

When he spun around again, Makena stood right behind him. She rubbed her hands over her arms. "I didn't want to stay in there with him."

Shane's gaze shot past her to the body on the floor. The guy hadn't moved, but he would, and Shane wanted him tied up and ready for questioning. He took out his cell to call in reinforcements.

She shook her head. "Mine wouldn't work for some reason."

Shane got a signal and sent the emergency code to Cameron Roth, one of his teammates, before turning back to her. "Stay here."

With the order given, Shane headed for the guy. Checked for breathing and was relieved the guy was still alive, because it was tough to question a dead man.

"Zip ties?" He knew she had them, but he asked anyway. No sister of Holt Kingston, leader of the Corcoran traveling team, would have a house without zip ties. The bigger question was why the attacker had stormed in here. He had nailed the door with a determined kick, and Shane wanted to know why. "Did he say anything to you?"

"Barely." She buzzed into the kitchen and came back with the restraints.

"I'm going to need to hear every word." Shane went to work on binding the unconscious man. "I'm guessing he was here to rob you, but with your connection to the Corcoran Team, we can't be too careful."

"He's not here for me. They…he…broke into the house next door." She paced the floor a few feet away from him. "I saw him, he saw me and then he came over here."

The idea of her being a witness brought him some comfort. Wrong place, wrong time. It sucked, but it meant she wasn't the target. That would help him sleep again…someday.

"Here." He handed her his cell. "Call the police. They'll need to check on the neighbors."

"I hate to think about what they'll find over there."

"You're not alone on that." Shane did a quick pocket check of the unconscious guy. He was about to stand up when he touched a piece of paper. Slipped it out of the guy's pocket and read the message. The words on it hit Shane like a kick to the gut.

She froze while pacing back and forth a few feet away. "What is it?"

"Your name and address."

She frowned. "What?"

There was only one explanation, and it chilled him straight to the bone. "The men were here for you."

Chapter Two

Makena tried not to throw up. Shane didn't spook easily. The guy tracked killers and kidnappers for a living. He waded into danger without blinking. But now he was crouched down in her family room, holding that piece of paper with his face turning pale and his mouth flattening into a thin line.

Without saying a word, Shane turned back to the downed man and ripped off the knit cap covering his face. "Do you recognize this guy? Have you ever seen him?"

Those qualified as the questions she could answer without even thinking about it. One look and she knew. "No. Never."

"Did he say anything that could—"

"Why is he here? Why my neighborhood?" That was all she could think to ask even though she knew the questions didn't make sense or even match what Shane was saying.

A guy in a commando outfit storming into

your house and holding a gun should raise a whole bunch of questions. None came to her in that moment. Her mind went blank. She chalked it up to some sort of weird self-protection mechanism.

She had no idea what her outward reaction looked like, but it had Shane standing up and reaching for her. His eyes narrowed as he stepped over the motionless body and put a hand on her arm. A touch she couldn't even feel.

"Let's try this," he said as he stood there facing her. "Take a deep breath."

"Okay." He could say anything next. She was willing to do or say whatever would unravel the confusion of the last few minutes.

"Did you tell anyone about Holt or the Corcoran Team?" Shane pitched his voice low as he asked, "Maybe in conversation or by accident? Even a mention of the team's name?"

It took a second for the question to register. She'd expected...something else. "No."

"It's fine if you did. I just need to know."

"I said no," she said, her voice growing louder with each word. She knew better. Corcoran's work depended on secrecy and the ability to move freely without being identified. They worked for governments and corporations, protecting and rescuing. She would never endanger anyone on the team.

And she would never risk Shane's life. Seeing him now, the broad shoulders and fit build that had his T-shirt hugging his biceps and hanging loose over his flat stomach, made her a little breathless. The short light brown hair and that familiar scruff around his chin just begged for her to run a finger over it. He possessed a handsome, almost pretty face that guaranteed an unending stream of teasing from his teammates…and she'd spent years loving him from a distance.

"It's easy to do." Shane shook his head. "More than once I've—"

"Honestly, Shane. No." She'd failed at a lot of things in her life, but not this. The safety of the people she cared about ranked above everything else. She'd never even stepped close to that line.

His gaze searched hers for another second. "I believe you."

"You should." It was almost insulting that he experienced any doubt.

"That leaves very few reasonable options." He stood so close and leaned in as he spoke. "Are you messed up in something?"

The words didn't make any sense at first. It was as if the slam against the floor had rattled her brain. Scrambled whatever up there helped her comprehend simple sentences. "Like what?"

"Something that would bring armed men to your door."

"Are you serious?" She worked at a desk. She read files and sat in on meetings. Nothing about her life shouted excitement…except for one thing. Her secret. The one piece she never shared. The same side work that kept her sane and would make Shane furious if he knew. She couldn't even imagine the warnings and threats he'd issue if he knew.

More body aches sparked to life the longer she stood there. She tried to take a mental inventory. Sore knee. A twinge in her back. That pain when she moved her wrist a certain way. She was going to be one big thumping bruise tomorrow.

"I'm being thorough." He talked slowly, enunciating each word. "We can't miss anything. Even the smallest bit can sometimes provide the lead."

"I work in college admissions. I can't really imagine a kid or a kid's parents resorting to this sort of revenge for an application rejection." Maybe she could, but that didn't mean they'd be able to find her. Neither her cell nor her address was public record.

But the other thing. She bit her bottom lip as she tried to reason it out. The part of her life, the private part, where she sat at a computer and conducted interviews. Pored through records and looked for lies. Those men could get angry enough to hurt her.

Shane stood over six feet and now he bent down until they stood eye to eye. "What aren't you telling me?"

"Nothing."

His intense stare didn't let up. "We've known each other for too long for me not to pick up on that bobble in your voice."

"I was attacked." But he was right. It had been years. She'd met him through Holt. Shane was her big brother's best friend. The guy with the bad marriage and, eventually, the difficult divorce. The one who made sure Holt came home safe from their assignments. The one who hung around and joked and looked and smelled so good.

For Makena, appreciation and attraction had grown from the second they met. She'd kept her feelings locked inside and pushed them away while he was married. Once he was single again, her gaze started lingering longer on Shane's broad chest. Even when they weren't together, the memory of his deep voice vibrated in her head. She looked forward to seeing him, even if the peek amounted to nothing more than a quick glimpse as Shane dropped Holt off somewhere.

She missed him when he was gone and enjoyed whatever little time they spent together these days. And today she silently thanked him for getting there on time. His entry had made all the difference. Anything could have happened to her if he'd waited a few more minutes to show up.

A groan cut off her mental wanderings. Low and almost a growl, it had her attention zipping to the floor. The attacker didn't move and his eyes didn't open, but the air changed. She felt rather than saw movement.

She shifted so they could both look down. "He's waking up."

"Good." Shane moved her back, just far enough that the attacker's hand no longer rested next to her foot. "I have some questions for him."

Funny, but all she wanted was to see the guy dragged out of her house and locked up. The *why* mattered, but seeing the guy's presence triggered a constant shaking inside her. "Any chance we could handle those at the police station?"

"I want to question this guy without an official report."

That sounded like one of those things Holt said and she tried to ignore because she did not want to know. "I'll pretend I didn't hear that."

Shane took a step in the downed man's direction and his eyes popped open. "You have two minutes to tell me who you are and why you're here." Shane aimed his gun at the attacker. "Or do you need an incentive?"

"Shane, please." The only thing she wanted less than to hear about Shane's work plans was to watch them in action. She understood the need for hard talk—even violence—to combat evil, but she did not want to witness it firsthand. She'd had enough of that tonight.

"Go wait outside for the police." He never broke eye contact with the attacker. They'd launched into a staring contest and neither of them moved.

She wanted Shane safe. She also wanted him to stay out of jail, so she was not leaving, no matter how much relief flooded through her at the thought at being outside in the fresh air and away from the injured attacker. "No way."

Shane shot her a quick glance before returning his attention to the guy on the floor. "I need answers. He has them."

The attacker lifted his head but didn't say anything. His fingers moved on the carpet and sent Shane's gaze bouncing.

He held out a hand in her direction even as his focus remained on the attacker's prone form. "Stay back."

She didn't have any intention of getting closer. The exact opposite, actually. She took one step and backed into a chair. She could add her calf to the list of injured body parts.

She swore as she glanced down. The room started spinning in slow motion. The attacker's foot hooked around hers and he pulled. Her knee buckled as the air whizzed under her. Prone one second, the attacker moved with record speed the next as he jackknifed into a sitting position.

Shane's hand brushed her forearm as he made a grab for her, but the attacker proved to be a second faster. He wrapped an arm around her legs. She fell and her weight came down in a rush. The next time she inhaled, she lay on top of the attacker, her back against his front, with the fire poker balanced on her neck, keeping her locked against him.

"Drop your gun." Those were the first words the attacker had spoken since Shane raced through the back door.

Her breath rushed out of her as her heartbeat thundered in her ears. The shaking inside her morphed into waves of panic. Tension filled the room and seemed to have Shane's arm locked as he pointed the gun just past her head at the attacker.

"I said drop it." The pressure against her neck closed in, choking off what little air moved through her, as the attacker spoke. "Do it or I kill her."

"No." Shane didn't offer anything else. Just that.

The attacker tightened his grip until his knuckles turned white. She could see his skin right by her face. His arms shook as he pulled in. The light began to fade on her.

No way was she going out like this, in her own home while Shane watched. She flailed, shifting her weight and elbowing as she pushed and kicked.

Shane said something, but she couldn't hear him. Couldn't hear anything. Could barely think.

Movement flashed in front of her. Shane went from looming over them to shifting to the side. A bang echoed through the room, right by her face. She felt the attacker shudder behind her. His hold tightened for a fraction of a second, then slipped away.

Her ears rang as Shane reached down and lifted her to her feet. She tried to turn and see what was happening as she rose, but Shane's arm blocked her. Her body came to a halt and her head rested on his shoulder as her leg muscles gave out. She glanced over his arm and spied the blood on the floor around the attacker's head, before she quickly closed her eyes again.

Shane had shot the guy.

The realization hit her and her stomach flipped. The trembling moving through her had her teeth chattering. "Did you…"

His arm tightened around her waist as his hand brushed up and down her back. "Yes."

The soothing gesture threatened to suck her in. She fought off the comfort and pulled back so she could look up at him. "You mean you killed him."

"Yeah."

He didn't deny it or try to pretty up the words. Part of her appreciated the clear voice and the sure way he spoke about his actions, without justification. But part of her hated how easy it all seemed for him.

"Are you okay?" With his hands on her shoulders, he turned her body until his shoulders stood between her and an unwanted view of the death below her.

She didn't see a reason to lie, so she didn't. "Not really."

"He would have killed you." Shane sounded so sure.

His conviction fueled hers. That fast, some of the haze cleared. "I know."

"Makena, I—" He broke eye contact and glanced toward the front of the house.

She heard it, too. "Sirens."

"Now we have a problem." Shane stepped back.

"Now? As opposed to two minutes ago?"

"Don't panic."

That comment almost guaranteed she would. "I doubt that."

"The police are going to come in here and act like I'm the suspect." He offered the explanation as he unloaded his gun.

"What?" She needed Shane right where he was. Not down at a police station. Not in danger. But that wasn't her only concern.

A new wave of panic crashed over her. The police could not go through her house. There were papers, folders and files they could not see. She hadn't done anything wrong, but she'd have to explain, and she couldn't. Not to them. Maybe not even to Shane.

He set his weapon on the table with the bullets next to it. "To be safe I'm going to get on my knees and—"

She grabbed on to his arm and fought to keep him on his feet. "No, I need your help." A frantic clawing ripped through her insides. "There are things here."

The sirens wailed and lights flashed outside the window. She could make out the shadows of people outside, likely neighbors gathered to see what was happening. There would be police and possibly press at some point.

None of this could happen.

Shane's hand went to her shoulder, then up to touch her hair. "Talk to me."

"The police can't go near my safe." She'd locked everything away in anticipation of Shane's visit. Gathered up every shred of evidence and hidden it. She knew if she'd left out even a piece of paper, Shane would sniff it out. She'd been so careful. And now…

His eyes narrowed. "What are you saying?"

"I'll explain later." She had his arm and started pushing and shoving him in the direction of the bedroom. "You just need to keep them away from the safe."

A banging started. Sounded like the side of a hand pounding against her front door. Then the doorbell dinged once, and then a second time. The noise hit a crescendo as her panic rose and whipped up around them.

"I'll keep the focus on me." He motioned toward the front door. "Go let them in."

"What about—"

"You'll explain it all later."

She didn't answer. Didn't have time because the front door crashed in. Chaos exploded around her as uniformed officers piled into her small family room. She turned back around to say something to Shane, but he'd disappeared.

Her glance dropped and she spied him on his knees, right near the body. He had his hands hooked behind his head, but the police kept shouting. They knocked him down on his stomach as they wrenched his arms behind his back.

"No, he's not—" A policeman pulled her back before she could rush in and move everyone off Shane.

Shane turned his head to the side and looked up at her. "Call Connor."

Her brain scrambled. "My cell doesn't work." She shook her head, trying to remember where she put it or why that information even mattered.

"They probably blocked the signal. Try again." He glared, as if willing her to listen. "We need Connor."

Connor Bowen, the owner and head of the Corcoran Team. The man with power and connections. She knew one thing: if Shane needed Connor for reinforcements, they were all in trouble.

Chapter Three

Shane tried not to stare at her. Being in the same room with Makena always resulted in the same reaction. His heart rate kicked up as fast as his common sense took a nosedive. The black hair, usually pulled back with those sexy curls hanging down by her ears. The dark eyes and hints of the heritage passed down from her Japanese mother.

The long legs and trim body…everything about her set his blood boiling. So beautiful that she tested every vow he'd ever made postdivorce about keeping relationships light and sex only. He wanted her every minute and fought off the attraction with every cell and every muscle.

He tore his attention away from her and watched his team as he stood in the middle of her family room with activity buzzing around him. Cam and Connor had arrived. Connor had walked through the door and immediately started doing what he did best—he ran the whole show. Came in with a cover and ordered people, all while silently wrestling control away from whatever poor schmuck thought he ran the crime scene.

Cam, along with Holt, formed the three-man traveling team for Corcoran. Cam showed up to help because that was what Cam did. No questions asked, he rushed in and provided support. Many times that included flying a helicopter. This time he stood on the other side of Makena, across from Shane, and made sure no one got near her.

Connor broke away from the detective and headed over to the Corcoran semicircle. "We have one dead attacker."

"Thanks to Shane," Cam said.

"You would have done the same thing." Every member of the team would have put his body in front of Makena. Forget about her being innocent, though that counted as a good answer. She was Holt's sister, and no one touched the people the team members cared about.

"Probably." Cam shrugged. "I'm betting I would have used more finesse. Maybe been quicker about it."

Shane knew Cam was joking...or engaging in what Cam thought qualified as joking. Making sly comments meant to break the tension. If Shane hadn't walked in on some guy manhandling Makena, watched as the guy tried to choke the life out of her, he might be more in the mood to be soothed. But not right now.

"The guy intended to kill me." The rough edge to Makena's words was hard to miss.

Cam's smile suggested he didn't. "Then I definitely would have killed him, too."

Shane was about to remind her about Cam's odd sense of humor when Connor broke in. "Now that we have that settled."

An officer behind Makena knocked into her. She jumped. Looked two seconds away from screaming but somehow managed to bite it back.

Shane could not help being impressed. She didn't deal in danger as they did, yet she'd stayed calm. She'd listened to the informal training they gave her and kept fighting no matter what. She never let down her guard. Those smarts and that strength had kept her alive.

She cleared her throat as she visibly brought her nerves back under control. Most signs vanished. All but the way she rubbed her hands together in front of her until her skin turned red. "What about my neighbors?"

No surprise her mind went there. Shane had checked on that first thing. "They weren't home."

Her shoulders fell as she blew out a long breath. "I heard a shot…or I thought I did."

She wouldn't like the answer, but Shane offered it anyway. "Killed the dog."

Cam swore under his breath. "That sucks."

An awful situation, but the death toll could have been so much worse and Shane remained grateful it wasn't. "At least it wasn't a person."

"I like dogs." Cam moved out of the way as the ambulance crew brought in the stretcher.

"Is this what you guys always talk about on a job?" Makena watched every move as the crew lifted the still body and locked the stretcher in place. Her voice shook and a certain sadness moved in her dark eyes.

Shane wanted to make it better. Fought the urge to go to her, put an arm around her...test his control to its very limit. But he would do it for her. Or he would have done it if the audience didn't consist of Cam and Connor and what looked like six police officers filing in and out of the house as the detectives talked in the corner.

Unable to think of the right thing to say, Shane went with the one thing that might help. "He's trying to calm you."

Her eyes narrowed as her head turned and she stared at Cam. "Really?"

"He's terrible at it. Makes you pity Julia, doesn't it?" Julia White, the love of Cam's life. The reason Shane now hesitated when he called in a favor or needed backup as he played a hunch.

"The office is working on background on the attacker." Connor talked over all of them. "Preliminary reports are he had a record. Petty stuff."

"Are we sure that's it?" Shane glanced around, from the discarded fire poker to the magazines strewn all over the floor. Despite the battle, most of the furniture and other stuff in the room remained intact. But the man was still dead. "If so, it looks as if he escalated this time."

Connor nodded as he retrieved his cell from his back pocket. "We need to call Holt."

"No." Makena put her hand over the phone. Looked as though she tried to tug it out of Connor's hands.

Connor pulled it out of reach. "Excuse me?"

Before she said a word, Shane knew where this was going to go. Holt had met Lindsey during a job. She had grown up in a cult but possessed an inner strength. Holt hadn't stood a chance against her. He fell in love in the equivalent of a week. He'd spent two months going back and forth from his house in Maryland to hers in Oregon, but he was on his way back home and bringing Lindsey with him for good this time.

"He needs to stay with Lindsey." Makena spoke slowly, as if she were explaining a big idea to a small child. "The only way he'll do that now is if he doesn't know this happened."

Connor waited until she finished. "That's not an option."

The stretcher rolled by and Shane moved the group to the side to stay out of the way. He also lowered his voice as the rumble of conversation in the room died down. "It actually is."

"This explanation should be interesting," Cam said under his breath.

"Makena can stay with me." Shane ignored Connor's lifted eyebrow and the stunned expression on Makena's face, though he thought she could play her shock down a bit. "For protection."

Cam cleared his throat. "Uh-huh."

"Protection?" Connor asked at the same time.

Shane decided to ignore both of them. "We need to move her to a safe location while we confirm this guy's identity and figure out why he had her contact information, because that suggests more than a burglary gone wrong."

"And you're volunteering to be her bodyguard." Connor hesitated over each word, not bothering to ask it as a question. "You think that's a good idea?"

"I'm standing right here." Makena rolled her eyes. "And I'm a grown-up who should be part of this conversation, in case you gentlemen missed that fact."

Shane could fight his team or Makena, not both. "Someone sent men after you and we need to know why."

"Because of Corcoran, I assume." Connor glanced at the detectives. "I've ordered a lock-down just to be safe."

"That sounds bad." Makena bit her bottom lip.

"My wife is not a fan of the protocol," Connor said. "No one on the team is, since it involves being trapped inside and having the women in our lives skip their regular schedules. Not exactly an easy task since they fight every minute of it."

Makena snorted. "Good for them."

"Easy for you to say." Cam whistled. "Julia is going to be ticked off."

Shane jumped back in before the conversation devolved into an us-versus-them battle. "You guys handle the lockdown and I'll handle Makena."

Her eyebrow lifted. "Oh, really?"

Okay, that was a miscalculation. He knew that tone. Dreaded that tone. "Your safety."

"Right." Cam nodded. "That's what you meant."

Connor shifted just enough to bring everyone's

attention snapping back to him. "I'll give you a twenty-four-hour reprieve on calling in Holt."

That was not going to go over well. Shane started a mental countdown. *Ten, nine, eight...*

"Don't I get to decide?" Makena asked.

"No." Connor's smile faded as fast as it came. "In the meantime, I need to go finish my 'Homeland Security is taking over' speech."

"That explains the uniforms." Makena's gaze roamed over Connor's vest.

Shane liked the Homeland ones. There was a certain subtlety to the white lettering on the dark material. Better than the FBI. The team had them all. Whatever the job called for, they were ready.

"I wear this, I flash paperwork and give out a phone number that rings in the office of a very important man, and we control the crime scene. No questions asked, which is what we need right now." From anyone else the comment would have come off more egotistical than realistic. Somehow Connor sold it.

Not that Makena was easy to impress. "That's a lot of power."

"I can be trusted." Connor winked and then walked away, forging a path as policemen shifted out of his way.

Cam waited a second, then followed. "I'm going to watch."

A crowd formed around Connor as he rapid-fired questions. Shane appreciated the distraction. Because it left him alone with Makena at least for a few minutes. Enough time had passed. He wanted answers.

"What's in that safe?" He'd kept the police interest off the bedroom and whatever Makena had locked in there, but he wanted to know.

She shushed him. Actually shushed him. "Not now."

He wanted to insist, but as his mind ran through the events of the past few hours, he couldn't bring himself to put her through one more thing. Not that they could wait long. Not with gunmen on the loose and a dead body being taken to the morgue. "Your time is running out."

Her eyebrow lifted. "Meaning?"

His temper. He'd had enough game playing during his marriage to last him forever.

With a hand on her forearm, he steered her out the front door to the porch. Neighbors milled around the yard, shadowed in the police cars' headlights. Darkness had fallen and a cool breeze carried the smell of the nearby river up to the cottage.

He ignored all of it and concentrated on her, making sure to drop her arm as soon as he could. Touching her just tempted him, and right now they had serious business to figure out. "You are way smarter than I am. You know what I'm saying."

She leaned in and dropped her voice to a low whisper. "Can you get it out of here without raising questions or causing a problem?"

He didn't even know what *it* was. He'd been to the house many times and didn't remember a safe. That probably meant a small one, which made his task easier. No way could he load a heavy safe on his back and get it out of there without questions.

"I'll be able to take the contents out." He made the distinction but didn't know if she picked up on it or not. "And when I do I plan on looking through whatever is in there, so don't even bother arguing about that."

She linked her hand under his elbow. "I should be able to do something to convince you not to invade my privacy."

The words skidded across his senses. She didn't mean...couldn't mean... "Don't do that."

Her dark eyes filled with confusion. "What?"

Doubt kicked him in the gut, but he ignored it. "If that's the kind of offer I think it is—"

She shot him a frown that suggested she was just about to kick him. "Oh, please. It was an honest comment."

"Before someone tried to kill you tonight, you would have just had to ask and I would have left your personal life alone." That wasn't quite true. His job provided him with the ability to check out certain details. If he thought she was in trouble, he would not have hesitated to rush in and help out. "But now that I know you're in danger and hiding something, the chance of you winning this battle is zero."

"You don't play fair." She waved a hand between them. "Whipping out that whole bodyguard, good-guy thing."

He had no idea what that meant, so he skipped over it. "Can we carry the contents?"

"Yes." The answer came quickly and didn't sound all that convincing.

But that didn't change the plan. He only had one real play here, and it depended on keeping Connor away from the usual full-house search. "We grab whatever this is, head to a dark and quiet place I know to get something to eat, and you tell me what the big secret is."

Her mouth dropped open. "You can eat after all that's happened?"

The woman latched on to the damnedest comments. "I can always eat."

"How is that possible?"

Shane couldn't remember the last time a situation had robbed him of his appetite. If it didn't mean more hours in the gym, he'd eat even more during the day. "I'm not exactly small."

She leaned against the porch railing. "Oh, I know."

She did it again. The husky tone. The potentially provocative phrasing. Much more of this and he'd hustle her out of there and do something really stupid. "Makena."

Silence screamed between them. After a few seconds she lifted her hands as if in mock surrender. "Fine. Sneak stuff out, eat and talk. Got it."

He could stick to that plan. He *had* to if he wanted to remain sane. "There, was that so hard?"

"Actually, yes."

A weight lifted off his shoulders. "Well, you better get used to it."

"The bossiness, the need you have to get your way—which?"

"All of it. Because for the next day, I'm all you've got." And for some reason, that made him feel infinitely better.

Chapter Four

Shane hadn't issued an empty threat. Makena could actually feel the time running out as she sat in a tucked-away corner booth of a diner she'd never heard of. Never mind that they were on her turf. Even with the out-of-control way he drove, he lived more than a half hour away. She spent all of her time in and around Chestertown. Yet he'd driven maybe fifteen miles and found some dive she never even knew existed. Drove right to it, so he definitely knew it was there.

"The owners don't spend a lot on lights." She squinted in the dark, trying to make out the faces of the diners sitting nearby but giving up. The smell of French fries and cheese lured her in. If the food tasted half as good as it smelled, she'd be back.

"It was just paperwork." He leaned an elbow on either side of his plate and ignored his hamburger. "That's what had you all twitchy."

Sounded as if Shane wanted to jump right

into work and the safe and her secrets. No. Thank. You.

She held up her sandwich. "It's actually grilled cheese."

He flattened a hand against the fake-wood table. "I know you're thinking you can drag this out, throw off my concentration."

She let the cheese stretch in a string before breaking it off and popping it in her mouth. "I'm hoping."

"No."

Energy pounded off him. Every line of his body suggested he'd nip and pick at this until he got his answers. The intense stare. The stiff shoulders. That determined punch to his voice.

She gave up and dumped the sandwich on her plate. "You do understand this has been a rough night, right?"

He frowned. "I guess. Sort of."

She thought about kicking him under the table but leaned in, dragging her body halfway across the table toward him, instead. "Did you miss the part where a guy died on my floor?"

"That sort of thing is not that out of the ordinary for me."

Scary thing was she knew he wasn't lying. Any sane woman would run. Take off in the opposite direction and not look back. She'd tried that. She honestly had. She'd dated other guys and pretended her heart didn't do triple time whenever she saw him. None of it worked.

The big tough-guy thing, the pretty face and linebacker body all combined to knock her off balance. She'd been attracted to him from the start, and the feelings refused to die. But right now she needed him to be more than the man she wove wild dreams about each night. She needed him to back off on her secrets but stay close in case someone really was after her.

She dropped back against the ripped booth and stared him down. "Your work scares me."

"It's fine." He waved her concerns off without ever breaking eye contact. "Back to our deal. I believe you have something to say to me."

She glanced up, about to tiptoe through the facts, when the words clogged in her throat. She could make out one face in the diner. Wasn't tough, since he walked directly toward her, in a line right behind Shane. Slow and steady steps with a face filled with fury.

A ball of anxiety started spinning in her stomach. She had to sit on her hands to keep from fidgeting. "Were we followed here?"

Shane picked most of the toppings off his burger. "You've been watching too much television."

She couldn't move. All of a sudden her body froze and her mind went blank. The guy could have a gun or…she needed Shane on high alert. "You don't understand."

Shane's expression changed as he shifted in his seat and glanced behind him. "What are you—"

The unwanted guest stopped right at the end of the table and stared at her. "Heard you had some trouble at your place tonight."

He looked far too happy about the idea. He'd also just painted a target on his chest as the lead suspect in her attack. "How would you know that?"

Shane stood up, shoving his way out until he seemed to take up most of the space around the booth. "Who are you?"

"You on a date with her?" Jeff barked out a harsh laugh. "Dude, you should run. This one is—"

"That's enough." Shane didn't even raise his voice. Didn't have to. The vibration of menace would have been tough to miss.

Jeff took a step back. "You going to fight me?"

"You do not want that." Shane shook his head as he eyed Jeff up and down. "Trust me."

The mood in the diner changed. People openly gawked and the waitress backed away from their table. Blame it on testosterone or whatever, but a battle was brewing and clearly everyone felt the danger. Except Jeff. He didn't back down.

He outweighed Shane by at least thirty pounds, but Shane was all lean muscle and lethal fighter.

This would be a bloodbath, and while Jeff deserved to be pounded into the floor, she didn't want to witness it. "Shane, stop."

"Listen to the woman, Shane."

"One more time. Who are you?" Shane's voice dripped with disdain.

"Just one of the men she screwed over." Jeff threw out an arm in her direction, nearly hitting her.

She pulled back just in time. "You can't blame me. You're the liar."

With each word, her anger rose. She seethed with it. This guy had tracked her down, showed up at her house more than once. He'd been in the wrong and now pretended to be the victim. She despised him and everything he stood for.

Jeff's face flushed red and he took a threatening step toward her. He reached his arm out but never touched her. Shane moved with lightning speed to stand between them and pushed the guy back. Kept pushing over Jeff's protests and swearing until his back hit the wall. Shane held Jeff there with a hand around his throat. That was it. One hand had him pinned.

Shane didn't even move as Jeff punched at his arm and moved his whole body, trying to break loose. When two men got up at another table, Shane held up a hand. Didn't say a word, but the gesture was enough to get them sitting back down again.

Makena's heart lodged in her throat and wouldn't slip back down again. She wanted to stop the madness, but it had spiraled so fast and so furiously and she could only stand there, openmouthed and stunned.

"We seem to be having a miscommunication issue here. Let me be clear." Shane's voice sounded deadly cold and even. "You don't go near her. Not to talk with her or touch her. Ever."

Jeff tried to pry Shane's hand off but failed. "She's been asking for it."

"That is the line said by every abusive male on the planet." Shane's grip tightened. "She dumped you. Move on."

The idea of dating Jeff made her stomach roll. "That's not what this is about."

Jeff scoffed. "As if I would date that piece of—" His words choked off as his eyes bulged.

"Last warning." Shane leaned in closer to Jeff. "If you think I won't rip you apart in front of an audience, you're dead wrong."

"Tough talk from a guy who doesn't even know what's going on."

It was as if Jeff wanted Shane to kill him. She couldn't believe Jeff missed the rage simmering there. That he couldn't see the darkness in Shane's eyes.

After a beat of silence Shane let Jeff go, but not before shoving his head back and knocking it against the wall. "Explain it to me."

Jeff doubled over in a coughing fit. It took him a few minutes to regain his composure. When he did, anger thrummed off him. "Ask your girlfriend. She's the one causing trouble." He scowled at her. "You going to turn on this guy, too?"

She hated being put in the role of bad guy. Jeff took no responsibility for his bad choices. That shouldn't surprise her, but it did. "Shane's not a liar."

"Makena, don't help," Shane said without moving his gaze away from Jeff.

"That won't work. She's ruthless."

Shane pointed at Jeff. "And you're done talking to her or about her."

He batted the hand away. "You'll find out. Just wait."

Makena watched as Jeff stomped off. Pivoted around the tables, ignoring all the stares and the waitress rooted to the spot with the coffee-pot dangling from her hand. The noise of the diner muffled. Makena could hear the creaking of chairs and the clanging of silverware, but it all sounded so distant.

Shane dropped back into his seat and stared at her. "So…"

"I never dated that guy. I would never date someone like him." She wanted that clear from the start.

The waitress darted over and refilled glasses. Shane waited until she left again to start talking. "What's his name? And do not hesitate. Tell me."

She didn't even have to wage an internal debate. It would all spill out now. "Jeff Horvath."

Shane exhaled. "And who is Jeff Horvath to you?"

"That's not exactly an easy question."

He shoved his plate of uneaten food aside and leaned in on his elbows. "Lucky for you, I have all night. All day tomorrow, too. Talk."

"He's a fake SEAL." The words tumbled out of her then. "You were in the military. Others weren't. There are men who pretend to be war heroes, special ops guys, and…they lie. They live their entire lives lying and not caring that real people fought and died doing what the liars claim to have done."

She expected to feel empty and frustrated at having the information pulled out of her, but no. A surge of relief hit her. She'd dealt with this huge weight and all the anger that came along with it for almost a year.

Shane's eyes narrowed and stayed there. "This Jeff is one of those guys?"

"Yes."

"Huh, I should have decked him." Shane dropped his hands to the table. Just inches from hers. "What does any of this have to do with you?"

This was the part he'd hate. She steeled her body for the inevitable yelling. "There's this website called *Wall of Dishonor*. It outs men who are pretending to be war heroes." When he continued to frown, she tried again. "I work for the website. Do research, file Freedom of Information Act requests."

"You work at a college. At a desk." His expression went blank. "Didn't you reiterate that earlier?"

The look on his face didn't fool her. He was winding up. She could feel the tension twisting the air around them. "Yes, but—"

"What, Makena?"

That tone. Not helpful, but she decided not to point that out, since he looked half-ready to strangle her. "I do this on the side."

"You tick off men who lie about military service. Men invested in their lies who have everything to lose when you uncover their deceit." With each word he jammed his fingertip against the table with a thud. "Do you hear the tone of my voice? Can you tell how bad this is?"

"They deserve to be exposed." She believed that to her core. She'd grown up with a military man. Her father had dedicated his life to his career more than he ever had his family. Early in his service, he'd been stationed in Hawaii and found the perfect military wife who put everything aside for his career. By the time Makena and Holt came along, their parents were entrenched.

Dad was tough and commanding and demanded excellence, something she'd failed at for almost all of her life. Holt had suffered their father's wrath while she'd been spared. She'd been the disappointment. She flailed and tried to find her way, but got something of a pass from her parents, who never expected much of her anyway. Holt went into the army.

She'd gotten a lot of things wrong in her life, but she understood the military mind-set and the sacrifices. She hated the idea of someone claiming to have served who never did. It was an insult, and she'd spent most of her free time for nearly a year hunting these guys down.

"I'm not denying that guys like Jeff should be exposed." Shane shook his head. "He deserves to be shamed."

"Then what's the problem?"

"You…are you…" He wiped a hand over his face. "Does Holt know?"

"No." Her big brother could not know. He would try to control her choices in the name of protecting her.

She understood the tendency, even appreciated the concern, but he had a hard time letting go of his protector mode and realizing she wasn't a kid anymore. The fact that she'd transferred colleges twice until she found the right fit and moved around in jobs until she landed at the college only supported his point that she was not responsible. But she was. She had a career now, paid rent. She had a purpose.

"You didn't tell him because you knew he'd lose his mind. That he'd forbid it."

Forbid. The word sliced through her brain, bringing a wave of anger right behind it. "I'm a grown woman. My big brother doesn't control what I do."

This time Shane slammed the side of his hand against the table. "He wants you safe."

There was a difference between safe and coddled. She wasn't convinced Holt, or Shane for that matter, always saw the line. "I get that, but he doesn't get to make choices for me."

Shane's back teeth slammed together. "I want you safe."

Well… Her heart sped up and it had nothing to

do with the argument. "I thought we were talking about Holt."

"We're talking about danger." Shane closed his eyes as he visibly wrestled to control the anger bouncing around inside him. "That guy talked as if he knew where you live. He was here, a place you said you've never been."

"Which is why I asked if we were followed." She'd checked, looked and thought they were safe...until Jeff walked in the door. The idea of him being so close and staying unseen terrified her.

Shane's mouth dropped open. "You're blaming me?"

That was not what she meant. Not at all. She put a hand over his, letting the warmth of his skin seep into her and wipe away the chill. "I'm admitting that I do this job. On the side."

"In secret."

"It's the only way to do it. The liars cover their tracks."

He opened his hand and let her fingers slide through his. "Let someone else take over."

She had to smile at that. "Says the guy who walks into danger every single day without asking someone to fill in for him."

"I'm trained for it. You're not." He turned her hand over and rubbed a thumb over her palm.

The move, so gentle and sweet, had something fluttering inside her. She forced her mind to focus. "For the most part I sit and look things up. It's completely safe."

"Then why does Jeff Horvath know who you are and how to get to you?"

The diner started spinning. She'd fought so hard to control her life, and one moment months ago had ruined all that.

"Because I messed up." She slipped her hand out from under his. "He was one of the first targets and I—"

"Targets?"

"—confronted him."

"You did what?" Shane's voice stayed flat and emotionless.

She looked away, but she could still see the moment. Filled with indignation and a sense of satisfaction, she'd stepped up to Jeff as he came out of church and told him, right there in front of his fiancée, that he'd been found out and now everyone would know. His business associates, his family, all the people he'd lied to for years, would know.

He'd claimed to be deployed while he played in Europe as a civilian. The tales of getting out early for some heroic act were even more ridiculous. She spewed it all in public instead of letting the website uncover him while she maintained her anonymity. A huge misstep she'd never made again, but the one time with Jeff was enough to keep her on edge.

She glanced at Shane again. Saw the rage bubbling under the surface and knew it was all for her. "Please don't break out into a lecture."

"I can't, because I'm speechless."

"You don't need to exaggerate."

His mouth opened twice before he spit out any words. "Do you have any idea what I'd do if someone hurt you?"

She'd waited forever for him to say something like that, and now he'd said it in a wave of fury. "No. You don't exactly share your feelings. How am I even supposed to know you'd care?"

"I'd care." He nodded toward her plate and the globs of now-cold cheese. "Fuel up, because we're going to spend a lot of hours talking about this."

She didn't hide her wince. "I was afraid you'd say something like that."

"You think fake military guys get angry? Wait until you hear this real retired army guy." He stole a French fry off her plate.

"I should have gone with Cam," she mumbled under her breath as she picked up her sandwich.

"Too bad, because you're stuck with me."

She wanted to hate that idea, but she couldn't.

Chapter Five

Under the circumstances, Shane thought he'd stayed pretty calm. He somehow choked down a burger and drove them to his house without wrecking the car despite the anger shaking through him.

The idea of Makena putting herself in the middle of so much danger made his head pound. He could feel the thumping through every inch of him and had to clamp his mouth shut to keep from yelling at her. Yelling or kissing...one of those.

"Are you ever going to talk again or is this whole brooding thing as good as I'm going to get this evening?" she asked.

"Excuse me?" She just didn't stop. Anyone should be able to see his nerves ran on the edge. Not her. She pushed and demanded.

He hated to admit it, but her refusal to back down from him was one of the many things he found so sexy about her. The face and how she looked in those jeans ranked pretty high as well.

She paced around the family room of his end-unit town house. The strip of houses sat up on a hill with a view of the Chesapeake Bay. He'd picked it because he could get to the Corcoran Team office in Annapolis quickly but didn't live right on top of the place like some of the other members. He needed a break now and then.

Seeing her there filled him with a strange sense of calm. She'd been there before, but always with other people. For group get-togethers. That had been on purpose, but now it was just the two of them. He tried not to think about the big bed upstairs, waiting.

She turned around and faced him while she rubbed her palms up and down her arms. "I get that you're disappointed in me."

Not that. Not even close. "Wrong word."

He actually viewed her secret work as brave and important. He just wished she didn't do it. The idea of her in danger, of some idiot who thought lying about being a SEAL was a good idea tracking her down and taking his revenge, almost doubled Shane over.

"I'm worried about you being involved in something that could get you hurt." He'd already blown it by saying he cared. He tried to write that off as the usual concern someone would have for his best friend's sister. Nothing more.

He knew better.

She waved a hand and shook her head. Neither seemed all that believable. "I'm fine."

"Yeah, you look fine." She'd paled until her skin looked white. And the way she hugged her body, wrapping her arms tight around her middle, said she'd reached her end. It was the only reason Shane hadn't launched into his mental list of a thousand questions.

"Admittedly, I'm a bit shaky." She sat down hard on the armrest of his couch. The room stayed mostly in shadows. The light over the stove in the kitchen behind her cast her in its glow.

"Getting attacked will do that."

Her leg swung back and forth as she stared at her hands. "And I fear you plan on lecturing me all night."

"We got the time, so why not?" He aimed for a lighter tone, but he felt anything but and the words came out harsher than intended.

She glanced up, pinning him with an intense stare. "I can think of better ways to pass the time."

He backed away until his heel hit the step leading up to the foyer and his front door. When he realized she had him running and jumping, he stopped. This was his house and he was in control. Had to be, and that meant maintaining his hands-off policy. "Don't do that."

"What?"

The smile. She knew. He'd bet money she knew. "Tempt me."

She shrugged. "Didn't know I could."

No way he believed that. She'd caught him staring at her more than once. The way she looked. "Do you own a mirror?"

"Do you?"

He went out of his way to never mention any casual dates with other women when she was around. With his past and his record with women—with his family's experience with marriage—she needed to stay in the hands-off category, but he didn't want to hurt her. No matter how he fought it, the attraction zapping between them went both ways.

"We need some ground rules." Seemed logical to him even though he had no idea what those rules would be except clothes on, no touching.

"Right." She sighed and got up. Walked around to the bottom of the stairs and stared up. "Are we staying here tonight?"

She made it sound as if they were sharing a bed, and that was not happening. He'd sleep on the floor and stay awake. He'd be sensible.

All good thoughts, but they scrambled in his

mind as he walked toward her. One second he stood in safety by the door. The next he waited one step below her with only inches separating them. Not a smart move, but his mind and body seemed to think otherwise.

"You're going to get some rest and then we're going to talk about your side job in the morning." She was going to hate this piece. "We need to fill Connor in and let him look into Jeff."

"Why only me?"

Sometimes she said something and lost him. Left him far behind her, coughing up dirt and trying to put the pieces together. "What?"

"Shouldn't we both rest?" She laid a hand on his shoulder.

He concentrated on the danger and ignored how good the simple touch felt. It burned him through the cotton of his shirt and had him squirming. "I'm assuming you're experiencing adrenaline burn off."

"Are you talking about that sensation of having balls bouncing around my stomach?"

Not really. "Sure."

"I did, but now I feel as if I could sleep for a month." Her fingers moved into his hair.

He somehow managed to swallow. "That's the one."

"Are you going to sleep with me?"

He hit the breaking point right there. They

were both adults, but she was so hot and tempting and…forget control. He dragged her off the step and down beside him. Before he could think it through or come to his senses, he lowered his head.

His mouth covered hers, and the ground shifted. He'd thought to wipe out the years of need with a quick kiss. Once and move on. Get back to work.

That backfired.

His mouth crossed over hers in a blinding kiss that had him wrapping his arms around her as his heartbeat hammered in his chest. Heat built between them, and a strange energy pulsed through the room. Forget staying detached and moving on. He fell in deeper. Tasting her, holding her, had every nerve ending zapping to life.

The noises she made went straight to his head. He debated taking her to bed and wondered how much they'd both regret it in the morning. The last thought had him lifting his head. He saw a flash of light off to his right and let go of her while he reached for his closest gun.

She stiffened. "What is it?"

"Visitors." He'd caught the beam from the flashlight, thin and bouncing as the holder walked. His gaze zipped to the front door and he saw another beam right before it blinked out.

Two attackers with enough training to know

to come in quietly and simultaneously. This was going to get loud.

Her fingernails dug into his arms. "How is that possible?"

Good question. The place didn't trace to him and no one had followed them, so Shane had the same question. But he'd worry about that later. "Go upstairs."

"Shouldn't we run to the car?"

Time to fill her in on the bad news. "The easy ways out are blocked."

"I don't understand."

"I think you do." He didn't have time to explain and she was smart enough to know exactly what was happening. She just didn't want it to be happening…and that made two of them. "Go upstairs and hide in the closet in my room. You'll see an extra weapon in the box on the floor. The bullets are hidden in the opposite corner."

"You keep a weapon in your closet just in case?"

All over the house, but now wasn't the time to go into that. "Go, Makena. Stay in there unless you see or hear me or one of the other members of the team."

"Right."

He grabbed her before she could spin and run up the steps. His hand cupped the side of her face. "I'm serious. Do not be a hero here."

Some of the haze cleared from her eyes and she nodded. "I get it."

The thump of her feet against the stairs echoed as Shane put his back against the wall. He had a knife and two guns within easy grabbing range, and that was just counting what he carried on him. Other weapons sat, hidden, nearby. Whatever he had to do to keep the attackers from getting upstairs and to her, he would do.

After a soft click, the front door opened. That would trip the silent alarm and send a scramble code back to Corcoran headquarters. On cue, the phone started ringing, but Shane waited. Not answering would have Connor moving in reinforcements even faster.

The entire team could come. Shane didn't care. He hoped to have the situation neutralized before then. One peek of a human and he'd shoot.

The crash of the glass from the back door shattering caught him by surprise. He ducked, unsure what had caused the break, a bullet or something else. When he lifted his head again, he spied the man stepping into his house. Shane came off the wall firing. The attacker's shoulder flew back as if he'd been hit, but he kept coming.

They had Kevlar vests on and he didn't, which put him at a distinct disadvantage. Shots rang out as he ducked. A second man came through the front. They had him pinned down and trapped. He couldn't crawl away or bore through the wall. That meant going upstairs. Bringing the fight to her. He hated the idea, but he had to keep moving. Standing still guaranteed he'd be shot.

In a crouch, he spun around the railing and started up the stairs, firing covering shots as he went. A simple mantra kept running through his brain—*aim for the head*.

Plaster kicked up around him and more glass shattered. He reached the top of the stairs just as one of the attackers started up behind him. Shane ducked around the wall for protection and concentrated on the steps. The thudding sound grew closer. He waited until the last possible second, then shifted and fired. Nailed the attacker right in the head and sent him sprawling backward.

Shane's breaths came out in steady pants as he scanned the downstairs, looking for the second attacker. The quiet hit him. The banging had stopped and nothing moved except for a curtain that caught the breeze from the broken window.

Too easy. They'd had him trapped and he got out. No way should that have happened without more bloodshed and a hail of bullets.

He heard a noise behind him in the bedroom and sneaked inside, gun up. His gaze went to the window. Nothing there. If the attacker had climbed in, he was hiding well. Too well.

The dark hair came first, sticking out around the corner leading to his bathroom and closet. Then Makena's face appeared.

"Are you okay?"

Makena whispered the question, but it echoed in his head loud enough to sound like a scream. With a finger over his lips, he gestured toward the window. He had to get her out, and there was only one way down from here.

He opened the bench under the window and took out the rappelling gear and held it out to her. "Here."

She stared at the rope and the carabiner, the locking mechanism that would secure her to the rope. "Are you kidding?"

"No." He opened the blinds, careful to keep the noise to a minimum, and glanced over the windowsill. The night was still on the ground below. He could see everything thanks to the security light he'd set up.

But they were running out of time. A second gunman roamed the house, and gunfire would bring people running. The police had likely already been called. His cover would hold, but Makena being at a second shooting in only a few hours would raise alarms. She'd be questioned, and Shane could not tolerate the idea of her sitting in a police station where he couldn't watch over her.

"We don't have time to argue." The rope was set up and ready to go, just in case. The sheer drop would be rough on him but impossible for her, so she needed the equipment.

He hooked the rope in position and slid it through the hooks that would hold it steady for her to climb down. They didn't have time for a sling and instructions. She needed to move.

With one eye focused on the door, he opened the window and shifted her until she sat on the sill.

She shook her head and clamped a hand down on his forearm. "I can't do this."

"Makena—"

She shook her head and her teeth chattered. "It's impossible."

"You can do anything." He glanced at her, quick but deadly serious. "You unmask liars as a hobby. You have more guts than most people I know."

"But I—" Her voice cut off and she ducked as gunfire pinged through the room.

"Hand over hand." He gave her a push. "Down, then run."

Just as her body slid over the edge, he ducked behind the bed. He had limited ammo left but another gun within reach. He could cover her as long as necessary.

Shots rang out for a few more seconds, and then silence. Shane looked up, took in the ripped comforter and shards of glass all over the floor. Dark clothing flashed in the doorway, then footsteps thudded on the steps.

Makena.

Shane raced to the window. She stood at the bottom, staring up. He didn't wait. With one hand on the rope, he dropped out of the window. He held his body weight steady for a second, descending at a rapid pace, then giving up and jumping the rest of the way.

He braced for impact. His knees took most of the brunt. He bit back a groan as he landed. That would hurt later, but he couldn't worry about it now. Snagging her hand, he took off, racing through the open yard at the back of the property to get to the parking lot. There they could duck in between cars and wait.

Their sneakers scrunched in the grass, then tapped across the concrete. Through it all, he never let go of her hand. He tugged, trying to keep the pace doable. She surprised him with her speed. Never complained or questioned, either. The woman impressed him in every way.

They slid to a stop by a truck and bent down.

Shane watched for feet as he sent the emergency signal to Cam. Connor could mobilize fast, but Cam tended to beat them all to a site. Shane was about to tell Makena how proud he was when he picked up the shadow. A man moving around the side of the building. He could go one of twenty ways, but he headed for them. Straight for them.

The attackers showing up at her house was one thing. People following them here was another. Impossible, actually. Shane knew subterfuge tactics. He could break a tail. But now this. It was as if they had a homing device in… He looked over his shoulder at Makena. A tracker. The first guy had planted one on her. Shane would bet on it.

He'd handle that, but first he had to take care of the newest threat. He wanted to take the guy alive. Bring him in and let the team question him. But then the guy prepared to fire, and Shane took him down. One shot to the head and he dropped.

But there could be more, so that meant one thing. He looked at Makena and tried to figure out the best way to say it. Then he just blurted it out.

"Strip." Even in the dark he could see her eyes widen. "I can explain, but I need everything off."

"Did you get hit in the head back there?"

Shane lifted his T-shirt over his head and handed it to her. "They're following you."

She took the shirt and held it up to her face. "So?"

A countdown ticked in his head. If a third gunman lurked out here somewhere, he'd be closing in soon. "Someone—I'm betting that first guy—planted a device on you that keeps bringing them to us, so I need you…"

She had his shirt balled in her fists. "What? Just say it."

"Naked."

She balanced on the balls of her feet and stared at him. For a few seconds she didn't say anything. "I thought you'd never ask."

Before he could answer—and he had no idea what he would have said—his cell beeped in his pocket. The noise and slight vibration made no sense until he remembered he'd already called for help.

When her fingers touched the bottom hem of her shirt, he turned away from her. Tried to block out the sound of clothes rustling and not think about what he would see if he looked over his shoulder.

He answered the phone instead. Talked before Cam could. "I need a cleanup crew at my house."

"That's the worst phrase ever." Her voice sounded muffled.

Shane ignored every thought running through his brain. Tried to ignore the fact that Makena stood a few feet away without any clothes on. This moment amounted to both his fantasy and his nightmare all wrapped up in one. "Connor prefers that term."

"And, of course, he knows people who do that work."

Shane could hear the smile in her voice. Let the sound wash over him. Could stand there for hours except for Cam saying his name on the other end of the line.

That snapped Shane back into reality and got him talking to Cam. "Meet us at the safe house by Foster's."

Cam would know that meant the old mill once owned by the Foster family. They had three neutral places close by they could go to if any team member hit the scramble warning. Connor made sure they always had options. Tonight, like so many times in the past, Shane gave thanks for his boss's compulsive tendencies and called the code for one of the safe houses.

"Is that code for something?" she asked.

This time Shane glanced over and immediately regretted it. The T-shirt hung down to her upper thighs. Not long enough to guarantee his peace of mind or prevent losing control.

The long legs, the way she curled her bare toes into the ground…he was a dead man. "And bring clothes for Makena."

Chapter Six

Makena took a deep breath as she stood in the bathroom of the safe house. The one-bedroom cottage sat at the end of a long, dark road. From the outside it looked broken-down and in need of repair. A building with fading brown wood and a crooked front porch.

Inside told a different story. Just getting to the front door meant unlocking gates and deactivating alarms. Shane did it all using his watch, and then led them through the door. The cozy interior consisted of a small kitchen and living area with an L-shaped sectional sofa. One door led to the bedroom with the bathroom tucked inside. The other opened into what Shane called an SCIF, a sectioned-off room for receiving and reviewing sensitive information. To her it looked like a bare room with a desk, computer and safe, and no windows.

Smoothing down the borrowed T-shirt, the same one that skimmed over her, and the sweatpants that were too long and puddled on the floor around her feet, she guessed Julia had handed Cam the clothing but decided not to ask. Between the stripping and the kiss, Makena's head still spun.

She stepped into the living area with a smile plastered on her face. Seeing Shane kicked up her heartbeat. Noticing Cam also sitting on the couch calmed her nerves a bit.

Cam looked up at her and smiled. "You look good."

"It was either this or a towel."

His smile deepened. "I'll refrain from saying anything in response to that."

"Good call." Shane sounded anything but happy.

Cam leaned back into the couch cushions. "Hey, you're the one to blame here."

"How do you figure that?"

"Clearly Makena being with you is putting her in danger." Cam frowned at Shane. "Why are you shaking your head?"

"Because you're wrong about that." Makena knew the back and forth could go on forever and decided to jump in. She walked farther into the room and took a seat at the very end of the couch. "This is about me, not Shane."

"You're saying that because of the note the

first attacker carried?" Cam exhaled. "Yeah, I get that, but there has to be an explanation."

"Yeah, someone is after her," Shane said.

"Not possible."

Shane nodded. "Totally possible."

They were off again. Somehow she managed not to roll her eyes at the male byplay. As much as she wanted to keep her private life private, she knew that would no longer be possible. Her connection to the side business led to a whole new list of suspects. "I do some work for this website called *Wall of Dishonor*."

Cam's eyes widened. "The SEAL-outing one?"

She took in Cam's show of interest and noted a bit of awe in his tone. The support came as a sharp contrast to Shane's reaction. "You know it?"

"Of course. I check it out now and then, and silently curse the liars who have their photos posted." Cam leaned forward with his elbows balanced on his knees. "You work there?"

"I do research and investigate. Corroborate the charges people lodge with the site about people lying about their service." It was a simplistic explanation, but going into the details about requests from the government for information and all the calls and contacts with people who could confirm the stories, or not, would bore them.

Cam nodded. "Cool."

"No, not cool," Shane barked out.

In case she hoped he'd changed his position, he dashed that. "Shane thinks I'm being irresponsible."

Cam looked at Shane. "Why? Those guys should be dragged out to face those who really did serve. Like you, for instance."

"It's dangerous," Shane said in a growling voice.

Since he'd skipped over Cam's point, she made one of her own. "So is driving."

Not that it had any noticeable impact on Shane. He kept right on talking. "Do you think Holt would like knowing she's doing this?"

"Is this really about Holt?" Cam almost whispered.

Exactly the question she wanted to ask. A man did not kiss like that, hold a woman with that sort of fierce grip, if he didn't think about her. At least she hoped that was true. "I've always liked Cam best."

Shane scoffed. "Get over it."

"Holt is in love with, and planning to spend the rest of his life with, a woman who dedicated the last few years to helping people escape a cult involved in gunrunning. How could he get upset about his sister having the same sort of bravery?" Cam asked.

For the first time all day Makena felt lighter. Some of the tension dragging her down eased. Hearing Cam give Shane a hard time shifted life back into perspective for her. "Well, Shane?"

"It's different when it's your sister." Shane shifted in his seat, and then did it again. For a man who rarely struggled with nerves, he seemed to be in a battle now.

Cam's eyebrow lifted. "Makena isn't your sister."

"This conversation is over." Shane emphasized his point by standing up. He walked into the kitchen.

She watched because she couldn't *not* watch. Something about the lazy gait that was anything but. "Because he says so."

Cam's amusement hadn't faded one bit. "Apparently."

Just as quickly as he'd left, Shane returned to the living area with a pad of paper in his hand. He scribbled something with his left hand. "We need to look into Jeff Horvath and—"

Cam frowned. "Who?"

"One of the men she exposed." Shane glanced up, but his expression stayed blank. "The same one who knows who she is and where she lives and followed us tonight."

"So he's behind all this?" Cam sounded doubtful.

"I'm not sure yet, but he's angry." Shane lowered the pages in his hand. "Out of control."

She bit her lip while she debated sharing the other part of the story. "He's also a bit of a stalker."

Shane's gaze shot to Cam. "Do you see what I'm saying about her being in danger?"

"You've made your point." And if he used the word *danger* one more time, her head might explode.

"I'll need a list of names of the guys you exposed." Shane flipped through the pages. "And the names of everyone you work with at the site. Work and personal contact information. The usual."

Only in his world did any of this qualify as normal, but she had a bigger problem. "Why?"

Shane didn't look up. "They could be in danger or part of the problem. We won't know until we start digging."

That was the problem. The idea of someone breaching Tyler Cowls's privacy had anxiety jumping around inside her. He would hate it and she could lose her position. "There's one guy, but he's really secretive."

Shane's head shot up. "I don't care."

"What kind of answer is that?" Not the one she'd expected and not reasonable under the circumstances. At least not to her.

"What's his name?" Shane asked, refusing to back down.

She tried a different approach. One even he couldn't argue with, in theory. "Let me talk with him and—"

"It's better not to tip him off, since we're going to see him tomorrow."

Apparently he could argue just fine. What a surprise. "Because you say so?"

"Yes."

Cam groaned as he stood up. "On that note, I should head out." He looked at Shane. "I need to talk with you for a second."

SHANE SERIOUSLY CONSIDERED refusing to go out on the porch. He sensed some sort of man-to-man talk coming and wanted to avoid it. "What's up?"

Cam leaned against the porch post and stared out into the darkness beyond. "You're blowing this."

"What are you talking about?" But Shane knew. He and Cam had talked about Makena before. All those years of thinking he hid his attraction proved wrong. Cam knew. He insisted they all knew, even Holt.

But wanting her and being right for her were two different things. Shane could not seem to get Cam to understand that.

"Nope." Cam shook his head as he glanced at his shoes. "You can't sell that level of denial. It's not believable."

He would never let this go, no matter how much Shane wanted that to happen. "You should go home and get some sleep and—"

Cam pushed away from the post. "Do you really think her working for the site is irresponsible?"

He loved her for it. That was what shook Shane so hard. How much everything she did resonated with him and how devastating it would be to lose her for good. "It's dangerous."

"So you've said. Repeatedly, which is annoying, by the way."

Maybe he needed to find a new word, because that one wasn't convincing anyone of anything. "Go ahead. Make your point."

"You care about her, and it's coloring everything you say and do."

Shane had figured that out long ago. "She's Holt's sister and we need—"

Cam groaned. "Stop."

"I'm not the marrying kind. Not anymore." He'd tried it once and it suffocated him. They had grown apart almost as soon as they walked down the aisle. Disappointment and hurt feelings led to a nasty divorce when it should have been easy. Shane remembered every soul-crushing moment. Remembered every vow he'd made not to travel down that road again.

"Who is talking marriage?" Cam didn't use the word *idiot*, but it hovered in the background.

"You think we could just fool around?" The idea sounded so good in Shane's head until he thought about the aftermath and how uncomfortable parties and every other group meeting could get.

"Maybe you should be asking her that, not me." Cam blew out a long breath. "Look, I know your marriage was a disaster."

"No worse than a few of my father's." Shane thought about the weddings…all four of them. His father didn't take much seriously, including marriage. He fooled around, lied, got laid off and basically ruined everything he touched. Shane fought hard not to become the man who had raised him, but the worry lingered out there.

"You're not him," Cam said, as if he'd heard the worry running through Shane's mind. "I know how this feels. You lose control and someone starts to matter more than anything else in your life. You make mistakes and bumble your way through them. I've been there."

Shane thought back to those early days in Cam's relationship with Julia. Cam, one of the most competent men on the planet, had turned into a complete mess. Shane didn't want any part of that. "Just because you and every other member of the team have paired off doesn't mean I intend to."

"She's not going to wait for you forever."

"She should be dating. Other guys, I mean." It hurt to say the words. He got them out over the sharp pain in his gut. Just the idea of her with someone else ripped him to shreds. He half expected to see blood on the floor. "I have to be careful how I deal with her."

"You could start with being supportive."

Shane closed his eyes. Just for a second to try to regain perspective and wipe the memory of that stupid kiss from his mind. "I don't want her working there."

"How do you think she feels about you walking into danger every day?"

Shane refused to think about that, because his job wasn't up for debate. He could handle it. He'd been trained.

"That's different." Though for a second he wondered if it really was. He fought for what he believed in. She claimed to be doing the same thing.

Cam shook his head. "You're headed for a tough fall."

"What does that mean?"

"You'll figure it out." Cam started down the porch steps. "Have a good night."

Shane stood there, watching the taillights disappear down the long drive. He wanted his mind to go blank and to have a moment without thinking or feeling. But the door creaked open behind him. He smelled the scent of her shampoo the second before she stepped out onto the porch.

"Did Cam leave?" She held on to the edge of the door as she peeked out.

Not ready for a civilized conversation, Shane tried to shut this one down. "I'll send him the list of contacts."

"I guess I should go write it, then."

He did that to her. Shut her down. Sucked the life and energy out of her voice. Acted like a jerk.

"Makena." He looked at her, drinking in the sight of her postshower. Dressed but still breaking his concentration. "You know I'm impressed with the work you're doing at the website, right? I'm just worried about your safety."

"I could tell from the way you were yelling and gritting your teeth together."

She had him there. "I could have handled this better. Not…you're not irresponsible. You're the exact opposite, actually."

Her head tilted to the side and her hair fell over her shoulder. "I've wasted a lot of time in my life doing stuff just because, being unfocused. Being a failure."

He didn't even know how to respond to that. That's not how he viewed her at all. "You're only twenty-six."

"I need to do this."

He knew all about need. He'd been driven to join the army for financial reasons and because he wanted a place of his own. "Maybe this isn't a risk worth taking."

"I have enough of those in my life."

She meant him. He got it. "I don't want to fight with you."

"What do you want?"

She couldn't ask that kind of question. It would open doors and send them down the wrong path. Being thrown together in close quarters would be hard enough without adding a new level of sexual tension into the mix.

"I don't know." The first time he'd ever lied to her. Right there.

"When you figure it out, let me know." Without another word, she turned and walked into the house.

It took every ounce of his willpower and strength not to follow her.

Chapter Seven

Frustration still ran through Makena the next morning, making her movements jerky and her head pound with a ceaseless headache. It had been a restless night. She'd taken the bed and Shane had switched off between the chair next to her and disappearing into the living room. Each time he left the room, she let out a breath of relief. Not because she wanted him gone but because having him so close and not touching him made her nuts.

"We sure he's home?" Shane stared at the green house on the quiet tree-lined Annapolis street.

"The house always looks like this."

"Empty?"

Makena couldn't exactly argue with Shane's point. The small house consisted of two floors. Had sort of a cozy dollhouse feel to it. Not what she'd expected the first time she met Tyler Cowls, retired navy guy and the owner of the

Wall of Dishonor website. The bottom floor had
a family room at the front and kitchen at the
back, with a small room in between that Tyler
used as a bedroom.

Upstairs housed the website office. An open
space filled with files, computers and boxes. The
neighbors would never know what happened
inside from looking at the cute space with the
white curtains.

"He's a secretive guy." They watched from
across the street and down a few houses. Shane
had insisted they approach with caution after
she'd called Tyler's unlisted number and hadn't
gotten an answer, something that never happened with Tyler. He was on call all the time.

Shane raised a small lens and looked through
it. "I wonder if Jeff Horvath knows where Tyler
lives."

She wondered how Shane would like to swallow that lens. "I've already admitted I messed
up with Horvath."

Shane dropped the glass and stared at her. "I
know. That wasn't a shot."

Yeah, right. "Are you sure?"

Standing there made her twitchy. She wanted
to argue with Shane and get him to open up
about last night, to admit the kiss had meant
something to him. But that line of conversa-

tion only led to heartache, and she needed clear focus now.

Talking to Tyler might help. Clearing this up and finding out if he'd been threatened could give them a lead to follow.

Shane grabbed her arm and pulled her back. "Hold up."

"Do you see something?" If so, that made one of them.

"Nothing."

"Okay, you lost me." Not for the first time and she doubted it would be the last, but it would be nice to have some idea what drove him.

"No movement at all." Shane glanced up and down the street. "You said he works from home and rarely leaves, yet there's no car in the driveway or out front. No shadows or signs of life in the house."

"He didn't answer my calls, either." Dread fell over her. Either Shane's question-everything personality had rubbed off on her or something was wrong. She hoped for the former. "We should go in."

"Me." He pointed at her. "You wait here and be ready to call nine-one-one."

She let Shane take two steps before delivering the news. "Tyler will never let you in. He doesn't trust anyone."

"Sounds like a nice guy." Shane took out his gun. "I'll depend on this to convince him."

"You think he doesn't have his own weapon?" With any other guy that might work, but Tyler would shoot first and not care enough to ask any questions later.

He suffered from a serious case of paranoia. He assumed most people lied. After serving in the navy and returning from Iraq with an injury, he believed in service and country and not much more. Getting him to trust her had taken a long time and many hours of drinking coffee at the shop near where she worked.

Shane swore under his breath. "Fine, but you follow my lead. We're also going to have a talk about your friends at some point."

Because that wasn't annoying or anything. "You want to be in charge of picking those, too?"

He actually smiled. "I probably shouldn't answer that."

She decided he was joking, or pretended he was, and started across the street at his side. They approached the house from the left with Shane constantly scanning the area. He didn't talk, but his intensity vibrated around them. By the time they got to the front porch, he had her nervous and doubting and worried. Something about having him on guard all the time sucked all the calm out of her.

She stepped up to the front door and dialed Tyler's number one more time, thinking to give him warning that she was about to ring the doorbell. She glanced over at Shane, expecting to see him inspecting the doorjamb for booby traps or something, but he wasn't standing there. Her hand dropped and she turned around. It didn't take long to pick him out. He paced the front lawn and stopped in front of one of the windows.

"We have a problem." He delivered the comment the way other people would read a grocery list, in an even tone. No panic.

That was fine, since she sensed she was about to panic enough for both of them. "Another one?"

"Is Tyler messy?"

The question didn't make any sense. "I don't understand—"

"Yeah, we have company." Shane raced past her, taking the porch steps two at a time and rammed his shoulder into the door. The wood cracked and the hinges creaked. On the second hit, the door flew open.

He stormed in and she followed. As soon as she stepped into the family room, her body froze. Ripped sofa cushions, smashed lamps. Someone had torn this place apart.

A bang sounded in the back of the house. She could see through to the kitchen and the open back door. Before she could yell to Shane, he was off. Her heartbeat sped up and fear clogged every pore. Oddly, she'd grown accustomed to the sensation—the rough breathing and anxiety slamming through her—and that scared her. She'd spent her entire life avoiding violence, and now it kept landing right in front of her.

She made it to the back door and stopped with her hands balanced against either side of the doorjamb. The backyard was empty except for the garage, and that looked to be locked. She needed some sign of Shane. To see his hair or those shoulders, anything to confirm he was fine.

But nothing bounced back to her but the usual sounds of a neighborhood. Cars in the distance and music playing in the house a few doors down. At least no gunfire. She winced and waited for it, but it never came.

"He's gone."

At the sound of Shane's voice behind her, she spun around. He stood in the open front door with his gun down by his side. Not winded, but the severe frown suggested he wasn't happy he'd lost the guy he was chasing.

"Did you see him?" she asked as soon as her ability to speak returned.

"Dark clothes. Male build." Shane closed the

door and came the whole way inside. "Nothing else."

She glanced around at the open kitchen cabinets and shredded books and papers all over the floor. It looked as if a hurricane had moved through, but they had a bigger problem than bad housekeeping. "Where's Tyler?"

"Good question." Shane's gaze went to the stairs. "What's up there?"

"Everything."

"I'm not sure what that means, but I'll check it out." Shane's sneaker hit the bottom step just as the back door flew open.

Makena felt the punch of warm air at her back. She meant to pivot, but an arm wrapped around her neck and yanked her body back. A gun appeared right by her head and aimed at Shane. Not that it shook him. He maintained a fighting stance only a few feet away, as if daring the attacker to shoot.

"Who are you?"

The male voice whizzed by Makena's ear and she nearly collapsed in relief. She recognized their guest, only he wasn't that. "You're okay."

Shane didn't even twitch. "Let her go or I will put you down."

The band around her throat eased, but she didn't step away. Not until she made sure Shane didn't put a hole in the guy. It was his house after all. "Shane, it's fine."

Tyler frowned. "Who are you?"

"The guy who is going to shoot you if you don't stand away from Makena."

There were too many armed men in the room. Last thing she needed was to step into the middle of a battle between these two. She held up both hands. "Okay, let's all calm down."

Tyler stared at Shane for another second before turning to her. "He's a friend of yours?"

That struck her as the wrong word, but now was not the time for that debate. "Yes. Tyler, this is Shane. Shane, this is the guy we're looking for."

Tyler finally lowered his gun. "No one should be looking for me."

Shane didn't reciprocate. "Too late."

SHANE HATED TYLER COWLS on sight.

Shane had expected an older man, an off-the-grid oddball type. Instead, he got a guy in the suburbs. Not some wild-haired conspiracy guy. No, Tyler was about Shane's age. Probably considered objectively good-looking with a serious staring problem, because his gaze followed Makena wherever she went.

Much more of that and Shane would punch the guy.

"Did you recognize the attackers?" Tyler circled his kitchen table and handed a water bottle to Makena before putting one in front of Shane.

"Thank you." She shook her head. "But no."

Shane continued to size up the other man. He had a name and now could start the team on a full investigation. If Tyler had a secret, Shane would find it.

In the meantime, they had a series of kidnappings and break-ins to resolve. "Petty criminal types."

Tyler stopped staring at Makena long enough to turn to Shane. "Tell me what you do again."

Shane really didn't like this guy. "I never told you the first time."

"Shane." The chair screeched across the floor as Makena pulled it closer to the table.

He bit back the wince when her heel slammed down on his foot. Fine. Message received. He could play nice on the surface while he ripped the guy's life apart behind the scenes.

"Recon work." He glared at Makena, letting her know that move wouldn't always work, before turning back to Tyler. "You're not asking about the break-in here. You don't even seem concerned."

"I saw the attacker coming, locked away what

I could and escaped out the window." Tyler pulled out a tablet and swiped his finger across the screen a few times. He turned it and laid it in front of Shane. "I like to be prepared."

Shane stared at the screen with reluctant admiration. Tyler had a security system that rivaled Corcoran's. Interesting choice for a guy who used to fly planes. "This is quite a setup."

"The people we expose are not happy to be found out." Tyler drew out the moment by taking a long drink of water and leaning back in his chair. "So I'm careful."

Makena lifted her hand. "Don't say it."

That was where Shane's mind had gone. Here Tyler sat in his house, all locked up with escape contingencies ready and a surveillance system that prepared him for the worst. Makena had a dead bolt on the door. Little did she understand how easy it was to break one of those.

But that was a discussion for another time... and they would have it. No way would he stand for her living without protection from now on. He didn't know what he wanted to install, but he'd figure out something.

"Which brings us back to the attacks on Makena." That was Shane's main concern. His only one, actually. If Tyler wanted to wallow in danger, fine, but he could not drag her down with him.

Tyler sneaked the hundredth peek at Makena. "I'd look at Jeff Horvath. Frank might have some other ideas."

Frank? Sounded like someone Makena had forgotten to mention. Another thing Shane planned to talk to her about later. "Who is Frank?"

She twisted the lid on and off her water bottle. "Frank Jay."

That triggered a memory, but Shane couldn't place it. "Why do I recognize the name?"

She didn't give him eye contact. Not while she picked at the label and otherwise attacked the poor water bottle from every direction. "He's on the site."

Shane grabbed the bottle out of her hands and set it on the table. "He's one of guys you exposed?"

Now he had her attention. She wore a wait-until-we-get-home scowl. "Yes, but he's redeemed."

Forget Jeff and Tyler. Shane's attention zoomed right to this newest information. They'd uncovered the truth about someone...then made friends with him? The shift didn't make any sense. "I doubt that."

"I've been skeptical, too, but he's done good work for us." When Makena finished her water,

Tyler passed her his and kept right on talking. "Came clean and is making amends."

"That makes your website sound like a twelve-step program." Shane said the first thing to pop into his head. It was either that or smash water bottles together. Tyler and Makena looked comfortable at the table. There was a quiet intimacy between them, as if they spent a lot of time together.

One more thing Shane hated.

"I think that's where he learned about amends." Tyler's eyebrow lifted as he talked. "I can put a list of other possibles together for you."

"Clearly this leads back to the site." Makena reached for Tyler's water bottle, then stopped. "The attacks on me. The break-in here."

Shane slid his bottle over to her while he talked to Tyler. Didn't even try to be subtle about the choice he offered her. "Who else knows about your connection to the site and where you live?"

"No one except Makena," Tyler said.

She froze. "Wait a minute."

"No, I'm saying the list of people should be really short." He turned the tablet back around and started typing.

"Maybe someone followed me here last week?"

She looked at Shane as she grabbed his bottle and took a sip.

"Possible." He tried to ignore the satisfaction surging through him and the quick glance Tyler took in her direction as she drank. "But why go after the two of you now?"

Tyler shrugged. "Someone finally put the pieces together and traced the site back to me. Then used Makena."

Not good enough. It all seemed too coincidental for Shane's taste. All the big security measures failing at one time? Unlikely. This was about something bigger led by someone with access to money and resources. Hiring criminals wasn't impossible, but the ones who'd attacked Makena had had skills. That took some knowledge.

"What happens now?" Shane knew how he intended to proceed with Makena's protection, but Tyler was the wild card. He could go somewhere or do something that unraveled everything.

Tyler glanced up from whatever he was doing on the tablet. "With what?"

Seemed obvious to Shane, but he spelled it out anyway. "Your address is known. Do you shut down the site and—"

"No." Anger seeped into the other man's voice for the first time since he'd lowered the gun. "I have other places to go."

And an unlimited supply of money, apparently. "Where?"

When Shane had Connor and the team check into Tyler, his finances would be on the list. A nice house in a good neighborhood, no full-time job other than the website, according to Makena, and now a safe house somewhere. Those kinds of preparations cost money. Connor had payments from their missions to set up what they needed. Big checks from big companies. Shane doubted Tyler had that sort of access to money.

Tyler smiled. "You'll understand why I'm not sharing that information."

Either this guy thought he was a Rambo type or he really was. Neither option made Shane feel any better about him. "We'll need a way to contact you."

"I'll give it to you. But that means the only people who know will be you. If something else happens..." Tyler stopped and cleared his throat. Even shrugged. There was nothing subtle about any of the gestures.

Makena's eyes narrowed. "What?"

But Shane got the point. Hard not to. "You think I'm behind this?"

"I don't know you," Tyler said.

"Funny, but I was thinking the same thing

about you." But Shane would. Within twenty-four hours he'd know everything about Tyler Cowls, and then they'd talk again.

Chapter Eight

Makena waited while Shane did his usual visual and physical check of the safe house. He looked under and over everything. Checked the traps he'd laid at the doors and windows to see if anyone had tripped a wire or moved a crumb.

He came back into the living area, tucking his gun away and dropping his keys on the kitchen table. Those long strides and the determined look on his face suggested he had a lecture just waiting on his tongue to be delivered.

She loved to watch him move, all lethal and stealthy. He stalked like a panther and rarely lost focus. But that didn't mean she was in the mood to hear him complain about whatever was on his mind. Not when she had a point of her own to make.

"You hated him." She meant Tyler, but she guessed Shane knew that.

He exhaled, long and loud, before lifting his head to stare at her. "Yep."

The force of his gaze almost knocked her backward. They stood on either side of the table with the furniture between them as a shield of sorts. She couldn't help but think they stood on the edge of a verbal war, though she did not know why.

"You didn't exactly hide it." Which touched off a bit of an angry fire inside her. That website meant a lot to her. Having Shane wave the work off as if it meant nothing put a bigger wedge between them than the table.

"Neither did he."

Something in his tone grabbed her attention. The words didn't sound right. "Meaning?"

Shane rested his palms on the chair in front of him. "He wanted to climb all over you."

A hiss escaped her lips at the ridiculous comment before she could stop it. "What are you talking about?"

His eyes widened and his mouth dropped. "Do you really not know this Tyler guy has a thing for you?"

But they were…he'd never… Her mind started spinning as the memories of all their meetings flipped past in her head. Talking over coffee. Meeting for dinner at his house. But she'd kept it professional.

Tyler had a boy-you-crushed-on-in-high-school look to him. Very cute. Friendly and charming. But she didn't feel anything more than respect for him. The older she got, the more she loved Shane. That had started blocking out her attraction to anyone else, making it impossible for her to move on. But Tyler didn't know that, and now she wondered about the signals she'd sent.

Guilt smacked into her. On top of the fear and adrenaline spikes of the past twenty-four hours, she could not handle one more emotion. So she packed it away to deal with later. And she would. She and Tyler. She'd make him understand.

"We work together. He's never made a move." All true, but now she wondered about the little things. The way he remembered her coffee order and made sure she ate. The glances he threw her. Why hadn't she seen it?

"Yet." Shane leaned harder against the chair. The wooden legs creaked and his hands balled into fists. "When he does make a move, what will you do?"

"We're not talking about this." Opening up about her love life with Shane could not happen. She needed to preserve some dignity.

He pushed off the chair and walked around the table toward her. "Are you interested in him?"

No, no, no. "Shane, you can't be this clueless."

"So, you're not."

Totally clueless. "Obviously not, as you should know."

"You're talking about the kiss."

She couldn't breathe. Could barely draw in enough air to speak. "It didn't mean anything to you."

"Did I say that?"

For every step he took, she took two in the opposite direction. They were all but ringing the table. She needed to leave. That was the answer. He could play this game on his own. She headed for the door.

"Where are you going?"

His question stopped her. She turned around to face him with her hands behind her, locked on the doorknob. "I need a walk."

"It doesn't work that way, Makena." Then he was right there. In front of her and so close. "I stay here. You stay here."

"You're the one I want to get away from." The words shot out of her before she could call them back.

Instead of being offended, he smiled. His hand caressed her cheek and he moved in closer. "Am I?"

She had no idea what this was or how to react. She knew what she wanted to do but went with dropping her head back against the door. "You've made it clear you're not interested."

"Now who's clueless?" His hands rested on either side of her waist, and his stance widened until his legs straddled hers.

"You practically ran out after we kissed." The comment came out as a whisper as she searched his eyes for some explanation of his sudden interest.

"That's not true." His fingers tightened on her waist. "But you are Holt's sister."

She'd known his name would come up. She could almost see the moment when Shane remembered his best friend and began the emotional push away from her. "Don't use him as the excuse."

"Fine." Shane put a hand against the door right by her head. Wrapped her in his warmth without touching her. "You're the commitment type and I'm a failure at that. What's the plan? We have sex a few times and then go back to acting like nothing ever happened?"

His words touched something deep inside her. She could hear the pain he hid underneath the sensible sentiment. He wasn't a man who failed at anything, but he viewed his private life as a war zone. His father failed at everything and ran through marriages. For some reason, Shane lumped himself in with the man who'd spent a lifetime ignoring him.

She put her hand against his chest and felt the thudding of his heartbeat. "Why do you think you're a failure at commitment?"

"I'm still paying off my divorce lawyer."

"Shane, no." When he started to pull away, she grabbed on to his forearms and held him still. He could have thrown off her hold, but he didn't. He stayed, and she took that as a good sign that he was at least willing to listen. "You guys were all wrong for each other. That needed to end."

Makena knew she walked a fine line. Patty had never wanted to be a military wife and resented every minute. Shane acted true to who he was, and this pulled them apart, to the extent that were ever really together. Makena wasn't convinced. She'd never seen a spark and he'd never talked about having a wife as anything more than a convenience…until it became very inconvenient.

"I made her promises about leaving the army and didn't." He exhaled. "I messed up."

She refused to let him take all the blame. Not after the whispers she'd heard from Holt about how difficult Patty could be. "You both did."

Shane shook his head. "How did we get on this topic?"

Because his marriage colored everything and

talking about it was inevitable. The question was whether they could pivot and talk about them without him bolting. "You seem to think I need a ring."

His thumb traced over her lips. "I'm trying to be responsible here."

Wrong answer. "Maybe I don't want you to be."

"Makena." He said her name like a plea.

"I am a grown woman." She wrapped her arms around his neck and pulled him in tighter against her. "This isn't about my brother or your ex or even your dad. This is about us. What we feel for each other."

His hands rubbed up and down her back. "If we start down this road—"

"Kiss me." Enough talking. They could talk this to death and never get anywhere. She was done with that.

His chest moved in harsh breaths now. "I won't stop."

"I don't want you to."

That was all it took. His mouth covered hers in a blinding kiss. The type that whipped around and shattered all control. She held on through the smack of heat while need pummeled her.

Her fingers slipped into his hair as she wrapped her body around his. The blood drained from her head, and a wave of dizziness hit her.

With an arm around her waist, he lifted her off the floor. She didn't fight the need to get closer, to burrow in deeper. She wrapped her legs around his thighs and held on.

He lifted his head. "Bedroom."

She couldn't say anything, so she nodded. Anything to hold on to the feeling and keep him from breaking away. She feared his brain would kick in and he'd go on the defensive. Shove her away. But none of that happened. He carried her through the small house, pushing the bedroom door open with his shoulder and carrying her inside.

Desire took off in a wild frenzy inside her. She held on because she never wanted to let go.

The room spun and her back hit the mattress. When she opened her eyes, he loomed above her, balancing on his elbow. She ran a fingertip over his eyebrow and across his cheek. Down to his mouth, then over that sexy scruff on his chin. "I love this."

He treated her to a husky chuckle. "That almost guarantees I won't shave it off."

The sound of his voice skimmed over her like a caress. The way he looked, who he was…she loved it all. "Good."

"Be sure."

She could feel his erection against her thigh and sensed the control it took for him to hold back and wait. But there was no need. She wanted this, wanted him. Had for what felt like forever. "I am."

He nodded and started to get up.

"What are you doing?" She grabbed him and tried to pull him back on top of her.

His smile remained as he leaned down and kissed her. A lingering kiss that left her breathless after he lifted his head again. "Condom."

In her haste she'd ignored the precautions. She was on the pill, but that wasn't the point. Heat hit her cheeks. "Right."

He winked. "The blush is cute."

He left the bed but only for a few seconds. She watched his back as she heard him root around in his bag, then he turned around again. He stripped off his shirt as his knee hit the bed. The mattress dipped and she rolled against him. Then he was on top of her, his hands everywhere at once. His leg slipped between hers as his hands snaked up under her shirt. When his palms touched the bare skin of her stomach, she almost jackknifed off the bed. When they ventured higher, right to the band of her bra, she stopped breathing.

His hands cupped her breasts, massaging and caressing before he lowered his head. He used his teeth to pull the shirt out of the way. One second she wore it and the next her hands rose and he drew it off her and threw it on the floor.

A mixture of want and need bombarded her. A warm breath blew over her as he peeled the material of her bra down and put his mouth on her. His tongue, those lips. It all hit her like a jolt to her senses. Her fingers slid through his hair and held his head tight against her.

Their legs tangled and her hands traveled down his back to his belt. She couldn't see, but she heard the clank of the buckle as she opened it. The tick of the zipper came next. He lifted his body off hers long enough to kick off his jeans. When he reached for his gray boxer briefs, she stopped him. Put a hand over his and guided her fingers to his erection. Cupping him, holding him, she tested every inch. Smoothed over his length.

He went wild. He shoved the briefs down and kicked them off. She had seconds to drink in the sight of him before he covered her again. His weight pressed her into the mattress as her hands ran over his skin.

When his mouth started traveling down to her stomach, she struggled out of her bra. By the time she rested her back on the mattress again, he was tugging on her pants. He'd gotten them open and now they slid down her legs. With the material gone, his mouth touched bare skin. He pressed a long line of kisses up her legs to her upper thighs. Between her legs. On her.

Her head fell back and her hands wrapped in the sheets as his tongue went to work. He licked and enticed. With each pass something inside her tightened. Those tiny internal muscles clamped down as her breath morphed into panting.

"Shane." She thought she said his name once, but it echoed in her head until she couldn't tell if the chant was real or imagined.

He kept kissing her, touching her, until her body felt inches from going up in flames. His hands pushed her legs farther apart. He slipped up, between them, until she cradled him. She heard a ripping sound and knew he'd found the condom packet where he dropped it on the bed.

He pressed against her, slowly sliding inside her, inch by inch. She blew out long breaths as her body adjusted to his. Then he was moving, pressing in and pulling out. The steady rhythm hypnotized her. The bed shook. The friction of their bodies sent her control crashing.

They touched everywhere. His mouth met hers as his body plunged inside her. When his hand slipped between their bodies, the tightness inside her snapped. Her body bucked and her legs clamped against him.

Her whole body shook as the orgasm overtook her. She lost all sense of time and felt the energy pulse through her. Heat rolled over them as sweat beaded on his shoulders. The waves of pleasure had just started to die down when his body stiffened and his head dropped down. He buried his face in her shoulder as he whispered her name.

It could have been minutes or seconds later when his weight pressed harder against her. He lay still as she threw back her head and struggled to regain her breathing. Slow and steady in, but it kept shuddering out of her. And she couldn't stop touching him. Her hands roamed over his shoulders and one skimmed up his arm.

He lifted his head and stared down at her. "Wow."

"Eloquent." She tried to bite back the laugh, but it crept out. She laughed until her whole body shook. When it finally died down, the amusement in his eyes matched the lightness running through her.

"No regrets?"

She shook her head as well as she could on the pillow. "None."

She waited for him to say something and ruin the moment. Ground her back teeth together as the dread hit her.

"Good."

Relief flooded her. "I think so."

He lifted off her and shifted his weight to her side, but their bodies never lost contact. He ran his fingertips across her collarbone and over her neck. The gentle touch had her nerve endings firing back to life. He'd exhausted her, wrung every ounce of energy from her, but could still bring her to want more.

But her eyes had different ideas. They started to close and she didn't fight it. She snuggled closer into his side and let the warmth of his body lure her in. "You feel so good."

"I was just about to say that to you." He pressed a kiss on her forehead. "Go to sleep."

She didn't have the strength to answer him. She thought she groaned, but she didn't know. Her muscles weighed her down and her bones refused to move. No body part responded to a signal from her brain. She took that as a sign it was time to sleep. After all the death and panic, her body gave in and she drifted.

She could feel him drag the covers over them. Smell his skin. She was just about to fall under when she heard him whisper.

"I can't fail at this."

Her eyes popped open, but she didn't move. Didn't want him to know she heard the fear. But she had, and now she had to figure out how to fix it.

Chapter Nine

Frank Jay had his orders. He'd gone from living one lie to another. Getting caught pretending to be a SEAL was just the start to his trouble. It led to the news story, then his friends turned on him and the two job offers on the table were rescinded. The interest from the senator who wanted a real-life hero on staff disappeared as fast as it had come.

No one wanted to be seen with him or associated with his name. Anyone who tried got an anonymous email directing them to *Wall of Dishonor*. The mistake refused to die.

His life had flipped upside down, and he took responsibility for that. That damn website also played a role, but he had created the problem. But what came after wasn't his fault. He'd apologized and gone to rehab. He'd been through the program and stayed clean. Hadn't had a drop of liquor in seven months. Seven long months.

Getting swept up in the rest had been an accident.

He thought about that as he sat in the coffee shop. His drink had long turned cold as he turned the file over in his hands. He'd picked it up ten minutes ago as ordered in the set drop location. Protocol demanded he finish the drink, get up and go, but he didn't. Not today. What else could they do to him?

He opened the fastener on the back of the folder and peeked inside. Photographs and paperwork. The usual. Digging deeper, he saw Makena Kingston's picture and a police report about a break-in at her house. He dropped the documents back inside, not needing to read more or wanting them to be seen. He'd been tied to enough conspiracies and trouble without adding more.

The bigger issue was what came next. He balanced an elbow on the table and stared blankly out the shop's window as he tried to reason it all out. He knew what the contents of the folder meant without reading closer. The boss wanted Makena dead.

Whatever she'd said or stumbled over put her on the firing line, and now... Frank shook his head. He liked her. After he'd gotten done hating her, which he had at first. The smug face and the way she'd scolded. But she'd been the first to believe him. She'd given him a second chance. And now she'd call and ask for help. Seek information. He'd give it to her, tying the string tighter. Then she would be gone and whatever secrets she had would get buried with her.

He took out his phone and stared at the screen. He was in countdown mode now. Soon his debt would be paid…but not soon enough to save Makena.

CAM ARRIVED EARLY the next morning. Too early. He used the alarm codes and buzzed through the layers of protection and walked in.

Makena stood in the kitchen wearing only Shane's tee. On her it worked like a minidress. Not that it fooled anyone. Shane could tell from Cam's smile and the knowing look in his eyes that he had figured out exactly what had happened here last night.

Shane cursed his unexpected need to sleep in. He rarely rested for long periods of time. With his history, short bursts of sleep with a hand on the weapon proved to be the answer. Not this morning. She'd wiped him out. The first time, the second… He'd finally fallen into an exhausted dream around three. Before that he couldn't leave her alone.

Makena unstuck from the floor as her gaze

traveled from Cam to Shane and back again. "I should probably...yeah, my clothes."

"Subtle," Shane mumbled under his breath, knowing no amount of subterfuge would help now.

"You're not exactly helping." She let her gaze drop to his briefs as she walked by.

Wearing only a T-shirt and briefs early in the morning wasn't odd, but wearing the outfit on a formal bodyguard assignment when Corcoran kept all kinds of gear and clothing there was. "Cam knows when to shut up."

"Let's hope so." She didn't turn around again as she headed for the bedroom.

Cam opened his mouth to say something, likely something smart, but Shane held up a hand. He gestured toward the front door. Shane got there first and did a check before opening it.

Instead of going out, he lounged in the doorway and crossed his arms in front of him. Waited for the comments he knew were headed his way. "Go ahead."

Cam nodded as he pretended to scan the horizon. "I'm just wondering if there's anything we need to talk about."

That was enough to answer. "No."

Cam glanced inside, toward the kitchen. With the door open, they could look from one end of the house to the other. That was the point of the safe house. It had to be easy to lock down and protect. All seven hundred square feet of this qualified.

He nodded in the direction of the closed bedroom door. "That looked pretty cozy."

Shane let his arms drop to his sides. "Do you want to die?"

"That's what I thought." Cam stepped around Shane and out onto the porch.

Puffy clouds rolled along the clear blue sky. The weather had warmed and the sun heated the porch. Shane ignored it all as he stood there in his bare feet. He'd never been ashamed of having sex and he wasn't about to start now. Not when it had been so good, so freeing.

Not when the nagging voice in his head told him he'd messed up. He didn't regret sleeping with Makena or holding her through the night. It was the way she'd looked at him this morning, all full of hope and renewed energy. As if she believed they could make something work, which was just the ultimate fairy tale.

He'd watched the male members of his family marry and then blow up every relationship in record time. They took advantage, lost jobs, drank too much. Shane had spent his entire life on the run so that his genes wouldn't catch up with him. The one time he'd tried to buck the trend, had found a woman who wanted out of her small town and tried to make a go of it, they'd both ended up miserable.

He couldn't do that to Makena and he sure owed more than that to Holt.

"You folded in about two days." Cam looked at his watch. "That could be a record."

Shane wasn't going to ask. He refused to ask. But… "What are you talking about now?"

"Only that it doesn't take a genius to figure out you stopped keeping your distance."

Shane's gaze zipped to the bedroom door. Still closed. He lowered his voice anyway. "Do I look like I want to talk about this?"

"You look like you got hit by a truck." Cam smiled, as he'd been doing since he walked in the door. "Good news is Connor is giving you a few more days."

"What are you talking about?" Shane wasn't leaving until the case was done. He didn't care what other assignments waited. He wasn't leaving Makena or dumping her off on another team member. The personal stuff had him reeling, but he'd see the other through. She would not be injured on his watch.

"Before he contacts Holt. He knows Holt is going to be ticked off for keeping the danger to Makena quiet, but Connor is willing to take the heat."

"Having her big brother rush back into town

and take over won't help." That trip would certainly make Shane's life more difficult. He'd been messing up things just fine without help, so, no, thanks. "We don't need to throw more people at this thing."

Biting down on his lip, Cam looked as if he was trying not to smile…and failing miserably. "Good argument."

Time for a topic change. That qualified as the easiest road out of this unwanted discussion. "Do you have information for me?"

"Yes." Cam hit a few buttons on his phone and then turned it around so Shane could see the photos on the screen. "You were right. There was a tracker in her pants pocket. Connor is tracing it."

Shane glanced at the photo and cursed himself for not checking for one the second after the first attack. He'd led her into danger by skipping steps. That was what he did around her. Work and safety and common sense all took a backseat to blinding need. And spending the night with her had not eased the burning inside him. He wanted her as much as—more than—he had before.

Sex never worked like that with him. He met a woman, stayed around for a few days, then moved on. But then this was not the usual sex.

"I'm guessing Connor is having Joel look into

all of this," Shane said. Joel Kidd, the tech genius of the group, was Cam's best friend. The guy worked magic with surveillance and had an eerie ability to find anything.

"The Jeff Horvath information is disturbing." Cam scrolled through whatever file he'd downloaded to the phone or whatever notes he had on there. "The guy lost everything when his face appeared on the site. Got fired. Fiancée left. Family isn't talking to him."

Not a surprise. Jeff had the angry-guy thing down. He threatened and postured and refused to back down even when common sense demanded it. "Sounds like motive."

"In worse news, he has skills. Has taken a bunch of survivalist courses and can definitely shoot."

That qualified as terrible news. Jeff had skills, and that, combined with the anger festering inside him, made him very dangerous. "It would have been easier if he actually went into the military instead of pretending to."

"Point is, Makena picked a bad guy to make an enemy."

Apparently she possessed a knack for that. When Shane talked to her about everything else once this case ended, he'd bring up that point, too. He'd never be able to survive knowing she lived her life without taking precautions. The website or no, she was Holt's sister and had ties to Corcoran, which made her safety a constant concern.

So did the men she knew, but Shane vowed to handle that part. "There's more."

That headache came roaring back to life. "You mean the other guys on the site?"

"Look closely at a guy named Frank Jay." He was a wild card for Shane. He didn't get the relationship or how the man had gone from foe to friend, but he'd figure it out. But he was not the main target. No, Shane reserved that space for someone else. "You should also do an in-depth search on the site's owner, Tyler Cowls."

Cam's eyebrow lifted. "I take it your meeting with him didn't go well."

"There's something about him." Shane actually didn't like anything about the guy, but the investigation would tell him what he needed to know.

"Anything specific?"

Shane heard the shower and knew Makena had dropped the tee and stepped under the spray. He tried to block the thought of her naked. "Tyler is in love with Makena."

Cam whistled. "That's a problem."

"No kidding." She protected the guy and he'd all but drooled over her. That made Shane the outsider, and he hated the sensation.

"I meant a problem for you." This time Cam laughed. "Did you tell him there's no room for him since you're already in love with her?"

And then there was that. The needling he'd get from his friends as more and more information about this case came out. Forget Holt—the other guys could handle the verbal battle just fine in his absence.

Since Shane didn't want Makena shutting off the water and overhearing something annoying, he tried one more time to get control of the conversation. "Keep your voice down."

"That's not a denial."

Shane hadn't even realized that had whizzed by him until it was too late. Probably better that way, as the idea of standing there insisting he felt nothing for her made something twist in his gut. "Just do the intensive background checks."

Some of the amusement faded from Cam's face. "We also need to know what case she's working on now, or just worked on. Someone tipped someone off and this exploded. I'm betting she's getting close to a piece of information someone doesn't want revealed."

Shane had been so lost in trying to stay away from her that he'd missed an easy check. Her work touched a lot of lives. The idea of a recent case setting this off sounded the most rational of all possibilities. "Makes sense."

"Of course it does." Cam slipped his phone back into his pocket. "You look awful, by the way."

The mix of no sleep and a whack of guilt did that to a guy. "Did I ask?"

"It's much more fun just to tell you."

Not for Shane. Nothing about this case or his time with Makena ran smoothly. He felt two steps behind and half out of it. A terrible combination for someone on bodyguard duty.

Not that he thought she was in danger around him. She wasn't. He'd dive in front of her if he had to, but his concentration kept getting tugged and pulled. Combine that with the confusing pieces of the case and the high risk of danger, and the worries of not being prepared kept pounding him.

He tried to put it all into words. "I have this feeling."

"Your instincts are usually pretty good, so what kind?"

He could pretty it up, but he didn't try. With Cam he didn't have to. They'd been through everything as a team, and Shane didn't play games with duty and team. Still, spitting it out meant giving life to the fear, and he hated to do that.

Cam's eyes narrowed. "Shane? What feeling?"

"That this is not going to end well." And it grew stronger every single day.

Chapter Ten

Makena thought meeting Frank in the park seemed a bit extreme, but he'd insisted on privacy and quiet. Shot down every suggestion that would have allowed them to sit down inside. No, he wanted out in the open, a fact that had Shane delivering an unending lecture for the entire drive over.

"Remember what I said." He slammed the door and stared at her over the top of the car.

"Don't wander, stay out of Frank's grabbing range and listen to you." Even she heard her dry tone. "Got it."

"This isn't a game." Shane came around the hood of the car and slipped his hand under her elbow. He didn't grab on, but his fingers didn't just skim her skin, either.

She didn't love it when this side of his personality came out. Protective and a bit controlling? Fine, she could handle those. Talking down to her? No. That was never going to be okay, and he hovered right on the line right now. It had to do with wanting her safe and worrying about her. She got that, but still.

"You think I don't know that?"

"This guy, Frank, pretended to be something he wasn't." Shane guided her through the parked cars and past the group of preteen boys debating which one of them possessed the better bike. "You can see where I might not believe his sudden change and claims of regret."

"You could try meeting him before judging him." Seemed obvious enough to her.

He stopped walking and brought her with him. There, under the lush canopy of trees with kids squealing in the distance, he stared her down. "I've met guys like Frank before. They rarely change."

The stiffness in his tone and stance bugged her. She refused to back down. Shane might bark and scare other people, but not her. She'd been standing up to him from the moment they met. He said he liked that about her. Well, they would see.

"What is your problem?" When he threw her a blank expression, she widened her eyes and stared right back with an *I'm waiting* look.

He glanced around, his gaze scanning the entire area before hesitating on a picnic table off to her left and then traveling back to her. "You are in danger and it makes me nuts."

No way could she hold on to her anger after that. "Oh."

His expression morphed from blank to frustrated. "*Oh?* That's your response?"

"Yeah. It's sweet." She knew she'd said the wrong thing as soon as the words slipped out.

"You're driving me…" He shook his head as the words cut off.

From the way he kept grinding his teeth together, she guessed the last word wasn't going to be good. She almost felt sorry for him. Almost, but not really, because he'd just admitted how much he cared. She knew he had a she's-my-friend's-sister loyalty, but this went deeper. The way he'd held her and kissed her, the way he protected her and reined in his temper even when he could have blown. It all told her she mattered. He might fight hard and play hard, but with her he took his time, and she wanted that to mean something important.

"Where is he?" Shane asked.

The question hit her from out of nowhere. She'd been thinking about him and them and what could be if he unclenched about the Holt issue and trusted her enough to believe in them together…and his mind was on the job. That summed up their relationship. Rarely on the same page except when kissing or in bed. Apparently talking was their issue.

"Frank." Shane nodded in the direction of the nearby picnic table, the one near the parking lot and about thirty feet away. "Is that him?"

She followed his gaze. Frank sat there wearing blue jeans and a baseball cap pulled low. "Yes."

Shane frowned but didn't start walking again. "He looks young."

"He is."

His hand slipped to her back. "Give me the details before we get over there."

She wanted to point out that they should have had this conversation in the car on the way over, but Shane didn't look open to discussing his decision-making, so she just answered, "Twenty-six. An all-American Midwestern-boy type. He was an army supply clerk who injured his back in a locker room but claimed to have fought on the front lines in Afghanistan."

Shane swore under his breath. "How did he get caught in the lie?"

"An anonymous tip to the website started me checking on his history. His claims all over social media didn't match up with the reports from anyone he served with." She remembered how easy his case had been. Her third and the one she celebrated the hardest because she'd done it alone. "His story unraveled from there and his hometown newspaper did a story."

Shane exhaled. "How do these guys think they can get away with it?"

"Some of them do." She lowered his voice. "Or they do unless the site or someone else exposes them."

They walked a few more steps in silence. They'd almost hit the edge of the table when he whispered one more thing. "You do good work."

The shock still gripped her when Frank looked up. She stuttered a few times before forcing out a greeting. "Thanks for coming."

He tipped his head back and stared up at Shane. "Who are you?"

Shane shook his head. "Not important."

"It is to me."

"He's with me." Makena slid onto the bench across from Frank and waited until Shane sat next to her to start talking to Frank again. "As I said on the phone, we need to ask you a few questions."

Frank shot a quick glance in Shane's direction before focusing on Makena. He reached a hand across the table. "I heard about your house. Are you okay?"

She folded her hands together on her lap. No way was she giving this guy mixed signals.

Shane jumped in and asked, "How?"

Frank frowned. "What?"

"How did you hear about the attack?" Nothing in Shane's tone suggested he had an ounce of patience left. His words came out in staccato bursts and he looked half-ready to lunge across the table and pounce. Probably would have done so if kids weren't playing on a swing set in the distance.

She decided to step in before she witnessed another bloodbath. "Frank, please. We need you to answer these questions."

He finally nodded. "There's an online group. Men who have been targets by the *Wall of Dishonor* website. They talk and someone mentioned you were in trouble."

"Trouble?"

Frank swallowed. "Attacked."

Her stomach fell. She could have sworn she heard it thud against the ground. A sick shaking moved through her as she tried to imagine the conversation and information these men shared. "So they all know where I live?"

"Not before the police were called in." He winced. "They do now."

She didn't realize her foot had started tapping until Shane put a hand over her knee. The touch should have soothed her. At any other time, it would have. But not now.

She knew these men and how desperately they

held on to their lies. How they viewed themselves as victims and took zero responsibility for
their behavior. Except for Frank. He'd stepped
up, but now that she knew about the loop and
his involvement… She kept her mouth closed
because she feared she'd start throwing up any
second.

Shane gave her knee a gentle squeeze. "Did
you know about the group?"

She could only shake her head. She'd almost
regained the ability to form words when a wall
of indignation smacked into her. The mix of fury
and frustration pounded off Shane. Sitting so
close, she could practically feel the fire burning inside him.

"Holding back information, Frank? I thought
you were all about making amends." Shane
didn't move, but he looked bigger, more formi-
dable. Somehow his body expanded and all the
air around them stopped, as if suspended. "You
understand how guilty that makes you look."

"I wouldn't be here if that were true." Frank's
jaw tightened along with his fists. Only the slight
bobble in his voice gave him away.

And Shane didn't back down. If anything, he
leaned in. "I'm not so sure."

"Who are you, again?"

Shane ignored the question. "Is anyone on this
loop taking credit for the attack?"

"No." Frank held up his hands as if he thought he could hold back the flood of anger shooting at him. "No, I would have said something. There was no warning. No one is admitting anything."

She almost hated to ask but had to. "Is anyone celebrating it?"

Frank nodded. "Everyone."

She really was going to be sick, right there where little kids played. She wanted to get up, pace around...move across the country. Somehow she stayed in her seat. Clamping on to Shane's hand with both of hers helped. Feeling his strength fed her. Helped her focus the rage and panic coursing through her at backbreaking speed.

"Except you, of course." Shane's voice dipped lower.

Makena knew that meant trouble. When his tone went soft, he hovered on the brink of explosion. This time she didn't plan to stop him.

"I'm trying to help here. I came when called. I've provided information on other men." Frank jerked in his seat when a dog started barking.

"Then give me what I need to look in on this loop." Shane took out his cell phone and swiped the keyboard.

The move seemed so normal, so every day, but something grabbed her attention. He didn't enter a lock code. She concentrated, studying the black rectangle in his hands. Yeah, that wasn't his phone. She had no idea where it had come from or why he had two, but now was not the time to ask.

"You can't just sit in or read along. This is a private loop and these guys guard all the information on there very closely." Frank's fidgeting ratcheted up. He looked around and leaned in. His hands kept moving.

Shane didn't show one sign of nerves. "I probably can, but just in case give me your log-in information."

"I...just..." Frank's mouth dropped open, and then he turned to her. "This is a dangerous game."

She got that now. Maybe at the beginning this had been an adventure. Never a game, because she took the work seriously, but she'd been excited about the research and uncovering information. The whole thing had given her a thrill. Now she knew how far some men would go to hold on to the lie they'd built, and it scared her.

"I'm the one people tried to kill. I'm well aware how dangerous this all is." She doubted she'd ever forget. She wondered if she could continue doing the work or take pride in any of it from now on.

Frank played with his hat, then scratched his neck. "Fine."

"Why are you so nervous?" Shane's eyes narrowed as he asked.

The question pulled her attention from the numerous little things and made her focus on the bigger picture. Frank looked ready to crawl out of his skin.

"You're not exactly the friendliest guy," Frank said.

No, it was more than that. Something bigger. She'd seen this guy at his worst, right after being found out. Over time, he'd changed. He got sober. He told people the truth. He delivered information, maybe even some of it from that private loop.

"He's actually being pretty civilized." And she wasn't kidding. Shane led with his fists. He'd been trained to ferret out the truth and punish liars.

She knew fury brewed and built inside Shane. The fact that he held it back and stayed coherent amounted to a pretty positive step forward.

"I'm not killing you for lying about being a big-time war hero, so you should consider this a good day." Shane spun the phone around and pointed to the blank notes section. "You're lucky, but I can't guarantee that will last if you don't cooperate and do it right now before I really get ticked off."

Well said. "Listen to him."

Frank coughed up the information. He typed it into the notes section, grumbling under his breath the entire time. He shoved the phone at Shane. "Here. Are you happy?"

Shane scoffed. "No."

"It's a start," she said at the same time.

"You should know there is a guy..." Frank wiped a hand over his mouth as he blew out a long breath.

"Get to it," Shane said as his voice sharpened around the edges.

She knew pushing too hard would stop the flow of information, so she trod a bit more carefully. After rubbing her fingers over the back of Shane's hand, she let go. Put her hand on the table in what she hoped came off as a supportive gesture. "Tell me."

"The owner of the group is a guy named Jeff Horvath." Frank gave one final look around before dropping his voice to a near whisper. "Be careful of him."

She talked over whatever Shane was going to say. "Why?"

"There's a core group of really angry guys, and he's their leader." Frank stared at his hands for a few seconds before looking up again. "He doesn't try to hide his dislike of you."

Not a surprise. He never had done so to her

face, either. Still, hearing Jeff's name sent a shiver of fear racing through her. "Okay."

"What else do we need to know?" Shane asked.

Frank started talking before Shane finished. "Nothing."

"That better be accurate." Shane put both elbows on the table and eyed up Frank. "You know why?"

"I don't—"

"Because I know where you live." Shane didn't even blink. "So, if anything happens to her, if someone comes near her, I'm going to assume you knew and didn't warn her. That for some reason you made the decision not to choke up the intel for me."

Frank shook his head. "That's not—"

"Then I'm going to choke you." Shane made it sound like a promise.

That was probably enough. She rushed in to get the conversation back on track. "Shane—"

Frank stood up. "I don't have to listen to this."

Shane rose, slow and deliberate, with each inch seeming to take a year. "Yeah, you do. That's the price you pay for what you did."

The nervous tics drained away, leaving behind only anger. A wall of it, from the angry red blush on Frank's face to his ramrod-straight back and stiffness in every muscle. "And just how long do you think I should pay for my mistake?"

Mistake? Makena couldn't believe the lack of self-awareness in that word.

"Forever."

She liked Shane's clear answer, so she didn't add one of her own. She stood up, ready to march back to the car with Shane. He'd launch into a lecture at some point, and in light of the information they'd just learned, she thought she might deserve one.

But they had to get out of there. Well, she did. If she looked at Frank for one more second, she might punch him just on principle.

"We should leave." She wrapped a hand around Shane's arm and tugged.

He didn't move. "Do you understand me, Frank?"

"Fine." He had taken two steps when the crack echoed through the trees.

Makena didn't understand what she was hearing, but it sounded wrong. As she turned toward the parking lot, where she thought the sound had come from, a pounding weight nailed her in the back. The world flashed in front of her as her body went down. She put out her hands and waited for the ground to smash into her face. But she felt a tug and turned in midair. Not by choice. Something moved her. It took a second for her to realize Shane had wrapped his body around hers.

She landed with a bounce against his chest. He groaned but didn't stop moving. He rolled her under him, pressing her back into the freshly cut grass and her face into his chest. She was about to ask him what was happening when the screaming registered. She heard voices and crying. Glanced up and saw people running. Then Shane's weight lifted.

"Do not move." He issued the order as he went.

She followed the flash of his body. In a few steps he hit Frank and knocked him to the ground. They both went down with Frank falling under Shane and neither man moving.

Tires squealed and sirens wailed in the distance. It took her brain another few seconds to kick into gear. A shooting. Someone had fired at her or Shane or Frank. Maybe at all of them. She doubted this was a coincidence and they'd just happened to be in the wrong place at the wrong time. Someone knew they were there or followed them…maybe Frank had been lying all along. The long list of possibilities made her dizzy.

Her gaze flicked to him. He lay on his stomach with his arms folded over his head. His whole body bucked as he said something she couldn't make out. Tears. The man was in a full-blown panicked cry. She sympathized. She also doubted a shooting mastermind would act like that.

Then Shane was by her side. He slid to his knees and pulled her up in his arms. His hands rubbed up and down her back as he rocked her. "Are you okay?"

"Is it over?" she stammered. She'd never tripped over her words before the attacks. Now she spent half her time trying to find the right word and spit it out.

"Makena?" Shane ran his hands over her. "Any injuries?"

Just from where he'd clunked her against the ground, but she didn't care about that. She snuggled closer into his chest. "I'm fine."

He held her for a few more seconds, mumbling soft words to her that made no sense but managed to soothe her. And she held on. Grabbed on to him with a death grip and refused to let go.

He finally let go, not seeming to notice she didn't. "I need to check on everyone."

"Don't leave me." She knew her answer came off as selfish and maybe a bit crazed, but she didn't care. Irrational was all she had right then.

"It's okay." Each word he uttered sounded measured and calm.

"No." That was all she could get out as she sat there all tucked and hiding from the world.

He slid that new phone out of his pocket and pushed a button. "Cam is on the line. Talk to him while I do a quick look."

He got away from her that time. Shifted to a crouch as he scanned the area.

"You could be killed." And that would destroy her. She'd lost control of her life, and the world kept spinning around her, but she knew that much. Losing him would rip her open until she'd never be whole again.

"The police are coming. Do you hear the sirens?" He caressed her cheek. "They are on the way, which would have made the shooter run."

Logical. Made sense. Unfortunately, she wasn't able to process common sense at the moment. But she tried. "You better be right."

"I am." He leaned in and kissed her. A soft peck on her forehead, more calming than heating.

He got up and went to a lady hiding under a picnic table nearby. Makena watched until Frank blocked her view. He scrambled over to her with a pale face and a drip of blood running down from a cut over his eye.

She knew she should rush to help, but all the energy had drained out of her. She sat there unable to move. "You're bleeding."

Frank touched his fingers to his head and

stared at the red on the tips. "From the guy knocking me down."

The words lit something inside her. This man had pretended to rescue. Shane actually did. "He saved you."

"I know. I was frozen." His voice sounded far away and stilted. "Could only stand there."

Realizing he wasn't arguing with her or blaming Shane sucked the rage right back out of her. "Me, too."

Some of the haze cleared from Frank's eyes. "Is that what happened to you the other night?"

She shivered at the memory and the new one that would haunt her for days...maybe longer. "Close."

"So this is all about the website."

Last week she might have let the comment pass. Not today. "No, Frank, it's about the men who lied and got called out on the website. One or more of them did this. Blame the right thing."

"We don't know that for sure."

"I do." She did. Knew it to her soul. She'd brought this danger into her life. She'd put Shane in peril. Shane and everyone in the park. Anyone who came near her. "And this time when they get caught, the punishment will be way more than public humiliation."

Frank's body froze. "What do you plan to do?"

That was easy. "Stop them for good."

Chapter Eleven

Shane couldn't shake the rage that threatened to plow him under. The men in Makena's life had her teetering on the edge of danger. He'd stepped out to give her space. To keep the need inside him from spilling out. The logic had made sense back then, but now he wondered if distance had done anything but cause more trouble.

He still wanted her. Kissing her, touching her, sleeping with her. It all had been so easy and felt so right. Then the bullets started flying and danger signs flashed and he fell back on the only way he knew to operate—he backed away. The cycle was making him nuts.

He blew out a long breath as he paced the parking lot. After the gunfire ended he'd performed a quick injury check of the people standing nearby. Most were shaken up, but none were injured.

Satisfied, he'd headed out here. Even now, police sirens echoed in the distance as they raced to the scene. Between the noise and calls from potential victims, an entire crowd of law enforcement should show up within minutes. Pretty soon he'd see the lights and then he'd lose control. If there was some piece of evidence to find, he needed to do it now.

Another glance in Makena's direction eased some of the anxiety slamming into him. She sat on the picnic table bench and watched over Frank and a few of the other people who roamed around, waiting for the police to arrive.

Frank…Shane couldn't place that wild card. The guy claimed to have some renewed sense of purpose after being exposed for the fraud he was. He acted as if he'd found a pool of integrity, but he possessed all the nervous tics of a man two inches from being caught in a lie. Not a good sign.

Shane vowed to wait and see what Connor's investigation turned up, but Frank had moved up on Shane's list of suspects. He did not trust the guy and certainly did not want him near Makena. Now was fine because Frank sat with his head down and looked ready to drop out of fear or guilt or whatever else was jumping around inside him.

Two Good Samaritans had the parking lot blocked off and were stopping new cars from pulling in. Shane had given them the directions and was relieved they followed them without question. Speaking with authority tended to work in these situations. Trouble made some people more willing to follow law-and-order commands. Brought out an inner protective streak Shane leaned on right now to keep the parking lot emptied out.

That allowed him to search. He kept up his pacing, up one line of cars and down the other. He wasn't clear about what he was looking for—evidence of the shooting or an idea of exactly where the guy had stood. He had an idea but would need Cam to come in and work some trajectories to be sure.

He got to the approximate spot. Cars took up most of the spaces, which made it a good place for a shooter to aim and then duck without a high risk of being seen. That didn't answer the questions about why here, out in the open, and who had been the target. Shane assumed Makena, but it could have been him or even Frank. Someone was intent on hiding something in this case, and who knew how far he or she would go to make that happen?

The scrape of a shoe against loose gravel had him turning. A footstep. Just one and then nothing, as if the person froze or dropped. Shane looked from one side to the other. Listened for any sound as he tried to pick up a sign of who else might be out there. That hadn't been a trick of his mind. He'd heard something. Someone close by.

Without making a sound, he crouched down. He didn't move so much as a pebble as he ducked beside the car and scanned the ground. He spied the visitor immediately.

Sneakers. Two rows over and one car down. He could see the blue jeans and the untied shoe. He waited a second longer to see if the guy shifted his weight or made a move, but nothing happened. He had the advantage, but he had to move fast.

Under or over. He debated for a second, only ruling out around because that would waste time and he could shift to one side while this person in hiding went the other way. Shane made the choice and moved. Slipped right over the top of the nearest hood and saw a head pop up. He made out the build and the hair as the guy took off toward the back of the parking lot and pic-nic area.

He swerved and wove as he moved. Shane went for the straight line. He didn't run through lines of cars, he vaulted over them, taking a row at a time until he ran right behind the guy. Two more steps…one more… Shane reached out and grabbed the guy's shirt. Got two fists full and jerked. Threw his weight behind it.

The guy lost his balance. Thanks to forward momentum, Shane crashed into the runner, causing him to stumble. With his grip secured and the advantage on his side, Shane heaved the man into the side of the nearest car and pinned him there. Nailed the guy across the shoulders and separated his legs with a kick.

Adrenaline rushed through Shane, fueling every move and giving him strength. He felt alive and on fire as he searched the guy for weapons. The energy continued to thrum even though he didn't find a gun. That probably meant he'd dumped the weapon, which was smart.

When Shane flipped the guy over and held him against the car with nothing more than a hand wrapped around his neck, his control almost snapped. He should have been surprised at the guy's identity, but for some reason he wasn't.

"Jeff Horvath." Shane didn't have to search his memory to call up the name, because this guy was also high on his list of suspects. Never mind that Frank had just pointed a finger at him. Shane hadn't liked this Jeff guy from the beginning.

"Let go of me." He squirmed and shifted all around.

Shane braced his arm across Jeff's throat and fought off the urge to press in hard. "Shut up."

The guy's eyes bulged as his fingers clawed at Shane's arm. "Stop."

"Calm down." When Jeff nodded, Shane eased up. He wanted to keep the guy slammed against the car but knew he had to back up. Actually doing that took another few seconds.

The minute Shane let go, Jeff doubled over, coughing and hacking. The display went on for what felt like forever. When he finally straightened up again, fury colored his features and he looked braced for a fight...until his gaze went to the gun in Shane's hand.

Amazing how a loaded weapon changed the balance of power. Not that it was all that level to begin with, but Jeff could pretend about that, too, if he wanted. The guy excelled at pretending.

"Let's try this again." Shane backed up a step just in case this guy was dumb enough to dive for the gun, thinking they could wrestle. Shane wanted to question him, not shoot him, but he would if he had to. "Why are you here?"

"It's a public park." Being the kind of guy he was, Jeff didn't back away quietly. He grew indignant and scowled.

One nowhere near his house, but Shane sailed over that detail. "Try again."

"I don't have to answer your questions."

Shane's gaze bounced down to his gun, then back up again. "This says you do."

Lights flashed as three police cars passed through the gate a few hundred feet away. The roar of the sirens grew louder, drawing everyone's attention. Everyone but Shane. He stood his ground and waited for an answer to the only question he cared about right now. "Why are you following Makena?"

Jeff glanced in the direction of the police cars. "I wasn't."

"They aren't going to help you." They actually would, because the diversion and their presence would stop Shane from going wild on the guy to get information, but Jeff didn't need to know that. "No one is."

The guy kept leaving a trail. He knew where she lived. He showed up after each incident. He'd made threats of a sort. If he'd wanted to paint a bull's-eye on his chest, he was doing a great job of it. And that was what didn't make any sense to Shane. It was too easy to tie the attacks right back to Jeff. He might not be a professional, but the file Makena had on him suggested he wasn't an idiot, either.

The whole thing smelled wrong and Shane couldn't figure out why. But he had a new problem, because she was heading right for them.

She didn't stop until she stood almost on top of them. "It was you? First my house and now you come here." She shook her head with a mouth twisted up in obvious disgust. "You could have hurt a kid or someone just walking by. What is wrong with you?"

She made good points, but this could explode. In addition to that, Shane didn't want her anywhere near Jeff or any other guy associated with the website. "Go back to the picnic area and—"

"We should turn him over to the police," she said as she moved away from Jeff to stand by Shane's side. "End this once and for all so I can get back to work and he can get the punishment he deserves."

"Woman, you just never stop." Jeff's hatred came out in the harshness of his voice and how he almost spit out the words.

"Do not talk to her." Shane shoved against the other guy's shoulder. "Ever."

"Not that it's any of your business, but I got a call to come to the park." Jeff sneaked another peek in the direction of the police. "I didn't ask for any of this."

The police parked on the far side of the lot, and the doors started banging as they got out of their vehicles. Shane started a mental countdown in his head. He couldn't be seen waving a gun around or he'd become a suspect.

He needed Connor to step in and get the place secured. He also wanted Jeff hauled away but knew that wasn't going to happen. The police might question him, but he should be able to squirm out of that cross-examination.

"We're supposed to believe you?" she asked.

"I don't care what you believe." Jeff tried to take a step toward her.

"Enough." Shane slammed the guy back against the car again. "Explain without the drama and bullying."

"Look at my phone." The guy looked in the general direction of his front pants pocket. "I got a text. Probably from her. This smells like a setup."

"You should continue to not talk unless I ask you a direct question." Shane slipped the cell out, scrolled through the messages until Jeff tried to grab the phone back, then concentrated on the texts.

The message was there from an unknown number. No name or identifying information. A simple statement and no reply from Jeff.

But that didn't make it authentic. Things could be faked. Alibis built on nothing.

"The message sounded cryptic, so I came." His gaze shot to Makena. "Just like you wanted me to. This was your plan, right? It all makes sense now."

She rolled her eyes. "You're forgetting that I was the one who was shot at ten minutes ago."

"And I'm sure you intend to blame that on me, too."

"No more talking." Shane's head might explode if this kept up for much longer. Every word Jeff uttered inched him closer to a punch in the face. "For the record, you lied about your military service. Be a man and own that."

"You don't know what you're talking about." Jeff's denial stayed strong, but some of the heat had left his voice.

"You're still denying?" Makena sounded stunned at the idea.

The idea didn't make much sense to Shane, either. He'd seen the evidence that Jeff had lied. No question about it. But getting him to grow up and take responsibility was not going to happen.

"I tried." Shane stepped back and gestured for Jeff to leave.

"Wait, what are you doing?" Makena grabbed Shane's arm.

"Letting him go." They needed evidence and they all had to get through the newest round of questioning headed their way. Once, maybe twice, Makena could sell the idea of being in the wrong place at the wrong time. Much more of this and the police's focus would shift to her. Shane needed to postpone that—hopefully avoid it, if possible. This case belonged to the Corcoran Team and it needed to stay there.

Jeff rubbed a hand over his neck. "I'm innocent."

"You're not, but if I find out you just shot at us, you will be dead." Shane put his gun away and made a mental note to check the parking lot for the shooter's gun since Jeff didn't have one on him. "Got that?"

"You don't scare me."

Maybe the guy wasn't as smart as Shane thought. "I should."

MAKENA HAD NO IDEA how she made it through the next hour. All those police questions. The sapping of her strength when she saw Jeff leave the lot. He'd been there, in the middle of her life…again. She didn't believe his phone or his story. She'd wanted to spill it all to the police and let them take him in, but Shane had said no. Then Connor arrived and backed up Shane.

She'd had just about enough of the Corcoran Team for one day.

After Shane did his usual search of the safe house before entering, she stepped through the doorway and kept going. She wasn't in the mood for mindless chitchat. She wanted a hot shower. Anything to wipe away the memory of the morning. Anything for a few minutes of quiet when no one tried to kill her. Seemed simple enough to her.

"What you do is important," he said in a determined whisper.

Shane's voice stopped her steps. It broke into the silence and dragged her back to the present. Had her spinning around. "What?"

"The work you do on the website." Shane dropped his keys on the table next to the small couch. "It matters."

This from the man who'd tried to talk her into leaving and had insisted she'd been foolish to help out there in the first place. She tried to put all the pieces together in her head and balance them against his comments now, and none of it made any sense.

"I don't understand what's happening." She stood frozen to the floor, staring at him.

"When you told me I wasn't supportive, you were right." He sat on the armrest. "I should have been, and I messed up. Meeting these guys..." Shane shook his head. "They're jerks and they should be exposed. They deserve whatever fallout comes to them and should not be able to just walk around as if nothing happened. You make sure that happens. You."

The heartfelt apology tugged at her. After everything that had happened and the exhaustion threatening to suck her under, she knew she should accept his words and duck into the other room. Get a little perspective and tighten the control. Rebuild the walls that held her back from saying too much. Her life kept rolling out in front of her, and now it included fear and danger, and she couldn't catch up no matter how fast she ran.

"I've spent my whole life trying to live up to Holt." The words spilled out and there was no way to call them back.

Shane frowned. "What does that mean?"

"He's always known what he wanted to do. He fights bad guys. He's not afraid or unclear." She loved Holt. He was a great big brother, but his greatness only served to highlight her flailing and years of uncertainty. "I'm the opposite. I bounced around colleges and jobs. I've never known what I wanted or how to get it. A path is so clear for other people, but not me."

"Not for everyone."

She noticed he didn't exclude himself. She got that. The military had been an escape hatch for him. His marriage had been about hope, not love. He viewed himself as so complex, but she saw through it all. She'd spent so much time deciphering him and his actions that little surprised her now.

But she knew her life, her choices, weren't as understandable to him. "The website was just one piece, and with it my life started falling into place."

Shane stood up and walked over until he stopped in front of her. "These insecurities you have. No one else sees you this way."

He refused to see the flaws, but she didn't have that luxury. "Ask my parents."

"They are of a different generation. They have whatever baggage they have." His hands rubbed up and down her arms. "Forget all that."

If only the looks of disappointment and constant reminders about all she'd failed to do with her life were that easy to ignore. But she tried to pretend. "Fine."

"You are this amazing woman. Beautiful, smart and focused." One hand went to her shoulder, then into her hair. "The idea that you can't see all you are and all you have to offer makes me want to shake some sense into you."

"I need you to see me as more than Holt's little sister." The sentence summed up her fears. That he would always look at her and see braces. See someone younger who followed him around with this crush instead of a woman who loved him for who he was, the scary parts as well as the good ones.

"It's a rough habit to break, but believe me when I say that is not how I view you anymore.

Not the only way." His hand went to the base of her neck and pulled her in closer.

"I need you to see me as a woman." Her head dropped back, cradled in his hand. "Living, breathing, feeling woman."

He didn't hesitate. "I do."

Relief had her gulping in breath. "I should have handled the website better. Protected my privacy and weighed the risks. I know I rushed in."

"You wanted to help." His gaze searched her face. "That is not a bad thing."

Every word he said, every touch, drove her feelings for him even deeper. She'd fought for acceptance her entire life. Her difficult parents had given up expecting things from her. Holt thought their overbearing nature was the worst, but their not even caring enough to fight about it ranked as the worst.

But Shane stood there, so open and loving, and told her she mattered. He accepted who she was, the uncertain parts and the focused ones. He didn't judge. Unless the other night had been an aberration, he didn't let any part of her past color how much he wanted her now. The words were freeing, and she grabbed on to them. Wrapped herself in that warm look he kept throwing her.

That only left one thing. "Any chance you're going to kiss me again?"

The corner of his mouth kicked up. "All night."

Her heart did a little twist. She felt the lightness and then excitement. They spun through her, wiping out every inch of darkness. "Really? I figured you'd do the that-was-fun-but-a-mistake thing."

She worried he would. Before he'd seemed to be looking for excuses to run away. He brought up Holt and the baby-sister thing all the time. But he wasn't using that excuse or any other now.

She was about to point out the change when he lowered his mouth to hers. His mouth touched hers, and a spike of heat hit her. Hands roamed her back, and lips covered hers. The kiss rolled on and her control faded. When he did that thing with his tongue, her knees buckled.

The touches lingered. Her body slid against his in excellent friction as she fought the urge to jump on top of him. Fought and only barely won.

When the blinding kiss threatened to go to her head and wipe out every sensible thought, she lifted her head. "Take me to bed."

He treated her to a full smile this time. "I thought you'd never ask."

Chapter Twelve

Frank paced around his apartment. That had been too close.

No one had told him to expect gunfire. He'd known something big was coming, something having to do with Makena and this new guy. He hadn't expected to be stuck in the middle of it.

Whatever clock kept ticking out there, it seemed to be winding faster. The tension rose along with the stakes. He couldn't handle any of it. He hadn't signed up for this. Yeah, he'd made a mistake, and he'd paid for it. Well, he thought so. Others didn't.

Ask his siblings or his friends, the few he still had. They all looked at him differently now. No one believed anything he said. Even when things did go well at the start of a new job, someone would find the website. They'd insist they'd stumbled over it, and another door would shut.

He deserved to feel bad about what he'd said. He didn't deserve to lose every piece of his life.

No one asked for the kind of pressure being applied now. Despite what Makena and her cohorts thought, no one deserved this type of scrutiny. It was time to move on and for his name to come down so his life could move forward.

He sat down on the barstool at his breakfast bar, then stood back up again. Unsure how much longer his legs would carry him, he dumped back on the cushion again.

A strange ticking noise filled the room. He glanced around, looking for the cause. He'd never heard it before and if he didn't track it down, it would drive him nuts.

His foot slipped off the footrest on the stool, and the noise ceased. Didn't wind down. It stopped. He glanced down and watched his leg. Realized it bounced up and down. His nerves were running on edge and the outward signs were tough to miss.

He put his foot back up on the rest, and the noise started all over again. The subconscious tapping made the far end of the footrest move up and down. Just a little, but enough to create the annoying sound. That was what his life had become, a series of random actions and weird noises.

He got up and started pacing again. He'd had two jobs today—give just enough information to get Makena worried about her safety and gather the requested information.

On cue his cell beeped. He reached for it on the counter and almost knocked it to the floor. The thing went sliding and he caught it just in time. Unlocked it and read the text. Didn't take long.

The number?

The main part of his assignment. Deliver the number. Frank had memorized it just to be safe. Shane and Makena had driven in and he'd watched. Sat at the picnic table close enough to get a good look. Good thing he'd done it at the beginning and repeated it over and over in his mind to memorize, because once the shooting started he'd been useless.

But having it and handing it over without knowing what the faceless person on the other end of the phone intended to do with it were two different things. He closed his eyes and when he opened them again nothing had changed. The text question was right there, taunting him.

From memory, he typed the series of letters and numbers in and then turned the screen off again. Now he needed to forget the number.

Because there was no reason for him to know Shane's license-plate number.

NONE OF THE background checks led to real information. Shane expected that of the men who lied about their military service. Many of them fabricated intricate stories, sometimes based on actual people's lives. Borrowed details and inserted themselves inside. And went to great lengths to sell the tales. There were personal sites and photos. A mountain of false information to comb through.

Connor had given Makena credit just that morning for wanting to do the work. Unraveling the information and finding corroboration and evidence refuting the claims of service could be a full-time job. Maybe that explained why Tyler didn't appear to hold any other positions or do any other work. It didn't explain why the under-the-table background investigation on him didn't check out. Some of the tales Tyler told appeared to be just that…fiction.

Tyler kept his life secret. He didn't advertise his service record on the website or anywhere else that Connor and the team could find. He had medals, because Makena had seen them. She'd also seen paperwork regarding deployments and other relocations. Problem was, Connor couldn't find the backup to support the stories or a way to replicate any of them. No witnesses. No government files. Nothing.

For a man who did a lot of finger-pointing,

albeit behind a wall of security without his identity being known, he didn't appear to possess a clean record of his own. On the surface, yes. Routine searches, even some more advanced ones, held up. But nothing about Corcoran could be considered routine, and Connor's access to information he shouldn't have, the internal security systems he shouldn't even know about, tended to stun them all.

The problem for Tyler was that Corcoran had intel it shouldn't have. That someone with something to hide would count on Corcoran not having. But the team did. It made lying to any team member tough, and it looked as if Tyler had done just that.

Standing in the middle of Tyler's small first floor, Shane was tempted to ask a bunch of questions. At the very least, go searching through the stacks of papers around here for information. But Makena stood next to him and he didn't sense she'd take either option very well.

Shane hadn't filled her in on his newest concerns. Not yet. He worried she'd have a hard time keeping cover. Or that was the excuse he told himself. He really worried she'd blame him for putting a microscope to Tyler's story. In the end he feared that if she had to pick sides, she'd go with Tyler.

"Are you okay?" Makena moved in next to

him with her arm wrapped around his as she crowded against his side.

Not that he minded the closeness, because he didn't. The smell of her shampoo. Her touch. The way she smiled up at him one minute and frowned at him the next. It all worked for him, and every single day his feelings grew deeper.

He pushed all that aside and focused on the problem in front of him. "Sure. Why?"

"You're standing in the middle of the room not saying anything." Amusement filled her voice.

He glanced around and didn't see Tyler. Didn't hear him, either. The small house stayed deadly quiet. "Where is your boss?"

"Upstairs…getting the information you wanted on Frank and Jeff." This time she did frown. "What's going on with you? You seem a million miles away."

He'd clearly missed part of a conversation. The lag had her worrying and him wondering what he'd missed. Rather than try to catch up, he pivoted to the conversation he wanted to have. "What case were you working on when all this started?"

"None."

The answer made no sense. He'd seen files and she'd been doing background work and fielding calls even now, over his objection, with all the danger bubbling up around her. "Are you afraid to leak confidential information to me?"

"Of course not."

"Really?"

"I thought you meant new work." She waved off the concern. "I have a few cases going on at the same time. Always do. One ended and I was about to look into another anonymous tip, add to the caseload."

Sounded fairly routine. Since the interest in shutting her down had seemed to arise all of a sudden and switched to relentless mode, he thought there must be a new case that had someone nervous. Sounded like no, but he decided to double-check. "Which name is that?"

She blinked a few times. "What does that mean?"

This conversation needed help. One of them still lagged behind, and he feared it was him. "On the list you gave Connor."

"I didn't." Before Shane could butt in, she rambled right over him. "I mean, the name would have been on Tyler's list. He took over the investigation. Said I needed a break."

Shane still wasn't sure he'd heard an answer, and now he really wanted one. "Do you remember the name?"

"I have it written down."

That was all he wanted. He didn't need to tiptoe around the conversation or worry about tipping anyone off. "I want it when we go back to the house."

Her eyebrow lifted. "Or we could just ask Tyler."

For whatever reason, Shane knew that was the wrong answer. "No."

Footsteps thudded on the stairs. The box appeared first, a good-size one that covered most of Tyler's body. He peeked around it as he walked into the room. "This is all yours. Everything I have on the men uncovered since Makena started working with me, including information on Frank and Jeff."

He dropped the box with a thud. Makena immediately went to it and started paging through the files. Shane took a break from the mental analysis for just a second and watched her. As she scanned every page, looked inside and touched each one, excitement lit her gaze. The work touched off something inside her.

He hated to hear her talk about herself as if her life hadn't amounted to anything or lacked some level of excitement, since neither point was correct. She had people who loved her. She held down a job and made a difference through her work on the site. She gave back by ensuring that only those who deserved to be were called heroes.

He admired everything about her. That drive she thought didn't exist, her compassion and charm. She looked like that and acted with integrity. He'd fought off his feelings for so long, pushed them back and hid behind a crappy marriage that never should have happened. He'd found excuse after excuse. Even made bets with the team and insisted anything other than sex was off the table.

He wanted all of it to be true. He hated the idea of being sucked in and having someone depend on him, only to leave her as he walked into danger. That was who he was, and that wouldn't change. It made relationships impossible. Apparently it didn't make falling in love impossible, because he had fallen. With her.

It couldn't happen and the odds made it impossible, but there it was. He loved her. Maybe he always had. He sat down hard on the kitchen table.

She rushed to his side. "Shane? All the color just left your face. Are you okay?"

No, he was very far from okay. "Sure."

"I don't—"

Time to dodge the question and get some answers. Shane looked at Tyler. "Who do you think is behind all this?"

"Jeff." Tyler shook his head as he grabbed the back of one of the other chairs. "You said he showed up while you guys were eating in that diner. He was at the park just now. I don't even know what to say about this loop with the other men that he told you about. That's news to me, but the lengths they'll go to sound pretty scary."

Clearly Makena had been busy filling her boss in. Shane understood why she thought that was okay, but he had a strange feeling it wasn't. Something about the guy didn't sit right.

Shane wasn't alone. No one on the team thought this was a straightforward case. Their collective experience and wisdom pointed to more than one person. Last thing Shane wanted was an entire group of liars with gun habits to battle, but the theory made sense.

Connor hadn't reached out to Holt to fill him in, but Shane knew their time was running out. That meant his time in bed with Makena likely was running out as well. If this couldn't go anywhere, they had to be realistic. Having fun when it was just them was one thing. They could keep that private. Rubbing Holt's nose in it once he got back did not sit well with Shane.

"What chatter are you picking up now?" Shane asked.

Tyler's grip tightened on the chair. "Chatter?"

"Reports about new cases." Makena smiled. "I think he's kind of asking how the work gets to us."

Shane did love her smarts. Tyler's blank stare was not a favorite. "You get leads all the time, right?"

"Yes."

"Are those drying up? Where is the business right now?" Shane knew most of this information from Tyler's financial records. The same ones that showed a sizable inheritance, which allowed him to spend his life chasing the liars on his site.

The questions weren't about scaring Tyler. Shane needed to assess the guy's truthfulness. Would he embellish or underplay? Would he even admit to knowing anything? Shane could get the information he needed or run into a wall that raised a red flag. For whatever reason, he sensed one of those outcomes was on the near horizon.

"I'm not sure I'm comfortable with this line of questions." The chair creaked as Tyler released the back and walked into the kitchen.

"He's asking for the case." Makena turned around in her chair. "This is all about the attacks. He's not going to steal your bank-account information."

"That's just the thing." Tyler walked back into the room with a water bottle in his hand. "We're assuming this is about you and this website, but from what I've seen of Shane I'm thinking he has some contacts that might be a problem for you."

Blame shifting. Shane knew that was rarely a good sign. "I need to rule everything out."

"I understand, but my financial life is not part of this." Tyler twisted the lid off the bottle with a loud crack. "These men are not adding to my bottom line. I don't get paid by the number of people we expose."

Tyler seemed determined to make that line of questioning into a dead end. Shane decided to let him. But now the team could rip this guy's life apart and Shane would not feel one ounce of guilt over it.

"Of course." He stood up and grabbed the box. "We should head out. It's been a rough few days."

Tyler almost looked relieved to know they were leaving. "No kidding."

Shane waited until the last minute to drop one more bomb. "Are you still staying here, or should we get in touch with you somewhere else?"

"No, here is fine." Tyler's smile didn't reach his eyes.

And that really didn't make sense. The guy had sensitive information stored at his house. No one was supposed to know who he was, and he was desperate to maintain that anonymity. Yet when someone broke in, he didn't ask for help.

He didn't pull up stakes or, at the very least, move the boxes somewhere else.

For a guy who supposedly felt as if he were in the firing line, he didn't act like it. He didn't show much emotion at all except maybe panic.

But Shane had gotten the response he'd expected, so he nodded. Put on his best we're-all-friends-here smile and headed for the front door. "We'll talk soon."

They had gotten out the front door and down the porch steps to the car before Makena whispered under her breath, "What was that about?"

"What do you mean?" No way was Shane answering that while still standing in the middle of danger territory. He'd taken a burner phone to the park as a precaution. He didn't want his cloned or lost, so he went with a fake one. It was just as likely he could be overheard. He had no idea what toys Tyler possessed, though he did intend to find out.

"Makena?" Tyler called out from the front doorway. "I need to see you on one more work issue."

Of course he did. So predictable.

Shane nodded in Tyler's general direction. "He wants you alone."

"Don't be so impressed with yourself. You are as transparent as he is." She leaned in closer.

"I know you're up to something. I can see the wheels turning in your head."

He would tell her later. Away from here. She'd yell and kick and scream, all while defending Tyler. So long as she didn't call him a hero, Shane could stomach whatever she said. "And you're wanted. Better find out why."

Shane would bet all the cash in his checking account that he knew what the topic of this conversation would be. Tyler had concerns. Tyler needed to talk.

And Shane knew it was about him.

Chapter Thirteen

Makena was not in the mood for a lecture, no matter who delivered it. Shane spent a lot of time giving her his opinion. Last night his words had lightened the guilt that had been weighing her down ever since people started dying in front of her.

Sure, she hadn't killed anyone and most of the men needed to be stopped, but the situation in the park could have ended differently. Violently. And every drop of blood tied back to her decision to take on her research work for the website. It was a lot to take in and almost more than she could handle. From the look on Tyler's face, he planned to give her even more to think about.

Tyler gestured for her to join him at the front door then put his back to the walkway and Shane standing twenty feet away by the street. "You doing okay?"

"Sure." But she knew that wasn't the question Tyler intended to ask. Not that she planned to make it easy. Nope. If he wanted to pry, he needed to go ahead and do it and risk her wrath if he went too far.

"This guy…"

She had to give him credit for jumping right to it, but her position hadn't changed. "Yes?"

Tyler shifted his weight from foot to foot. His gaze kept bouncing to the front door as if he expected Shane to come barging in. "How much do you know about him?"

She didn't need to ask for specifics. She knew Tyler was talking about Shane. "Everything."

Tyler's eyes narrowed. "Excuse me?"

No way was she spelling that out. "I've known him for years."

"Known, as in…" When she just stood there, Tyler's fidgeting increased. Much more of this and he'd be dancing down the street. "You two aren't together?"

Interesting phrasing. "Why are you asking?"

"I'm concerned."

"Why?"

Tyler smacked his lips together and glanced off to his left. He acted as if he tasted each word before he said it. "He's a bit rough for you."

She had no idea what that meant. Wasn't sure she wanted to know. "My feelings for Shane are personal."

"But you do have feelings for him?"

She didn't see a reason to lie. Even Shane knew about this at some level. "Yes."

Tyler shook his head, then did it again. Didn't say anything for a few seconds.

She touched her hand to his arm. "I appreciate that you worry about me."

"Of course I do."

Just what she needed, another man in her life who wanted to tuck her away in a closet to keep her safe. Maybe a week ago she would have been grateful. Now the overabundance of caution insulted her a little. She'd faced tragedy and death over the past few days and hadn't folded. She was stronger than any of them knew. Stronger than she'd ever known.

Only Shane seemed to get it. He didn't try to pack her away or send her to Holt. He kept her by his side and claimed to understand she needed space, but she also needed to see her decision about working on the website through to the end.

"Shane and I…" She fought to find the right words. "We get each other. He'll keep you safe."

Tyler slid a hand over hers. "I can keep me and you safe."

The vibe changed and her comfort level dropped. She'd worked side by side with this man for a year. They shared information and jokes, talked via text and on the computer. They spent far less time together because of her full-time work schedule, but they had shared meals.

To her it all related to business and a friend-ship. Now she wondered if Shane was right and if, for Tyler, all those times together amounted to something more.

Guilt knocked into her. A different kind, per-sonal and twisting. She'd never meant to lead him on. Shane had her heart, even if he hadn't shown any signs until recently of even want-ing it.

She slipped her hand out from under his and dropped her arms to her sides. "I'm good with Shane."

"You should—"

"Are you ready to go?" Shane stalked up the walkway toward them and the front door. "It's not a great idea to be standing out here in the open after the days you've had."

Such a subtle guy. She'd bet he'd been listen-ing to every word. His skills appeared to be end-less. Superhearing could easily be one of them.

"We were talking about work." She lied only to save Tyler from any embarrassment. Maybe men didn't work that way, but she didn't want to test the issue.

Shane smiled as he walked up the steps to join them. "I figured."

"We have some work we need to get done,"

Tyler said. "You could come back or I could drop her off at—"

"No," Shane answered right before she could give the same response.

Tyler's sudden possessiveness creeped her out. She suspected the feelings were new and innocent, but something about his energy felt off. After all those lunches together, she didn't want to be alone with him, and they certainly didn't have work. If he expected to spend a few hours berating Shane, Tyler had the wrong audience.

"I think Makena should get to make that decision." Tyler crossed his arms in front of him, looking far more confident in his position than he should have.

"Right. Good point." Shane turned to her, the amusement obvious in the way his mouth inched up at the edges. "Makena, you pick which one of us you want to be with."

Talk about a loaded comment. Not that her answer was in question. This, their relationship, only played out one way. She loved Shane. He was her forever. If he didn't figure that out soon, she'd have to move on and settle for less than she wanted. The idea of that happening hollowed out her stomach, leaving her raw and twitchy.

Her gaze zipped between the two men in front of her. One with the ego she didn't want to bruise and the other who needed to stop taking her for granted. Not that there was really any contest. "I'm leaving with Shane."

Tyler shook his head. "But we need—"

"You heard her." Shane winked at her. "Ready to go?"

For a second she wished she could love someone else. Someone easier. "We'll let you know what we hear about the park and anything we uncover."

Makena didn't look at Tyler again as she walked with Shane. They'd parked a short distance away just to be safe and the silence made the walk back feel even longer. She waited until Shane stood beside her near the front of the car to whisper, "You don't have to be a jerk to Tyler."

"He's alive, ain't he?"

He sounded far too amused for her liking. "Why do I think you actually believe that's an answer?"

"Because we know each other so well." He followed her to her side of the car and opened the door for her. "Isn't that what you told him? We get each other?"

"You were listening." Not a question, because she didn't need to ask. She knew and had expected all along.

"Do you blame me?"

She slid into the seat and glanced up at him. "Your ego will be unbearable now."

He leaned in with a wide smile plastered on his face. "Blame yourself."

TWENTY MINUTES LATER, Shane understood Makena was not amused. She hadn't said a word since they pulled away from the curb at Tyler's house. Just stared out the window, tracing a finger over the glass, humming now and then. Not talking to him or even looking at him, which he found annoying.

Shane decided to put it out there. State what ate at him. Not Tyler's murky past or questionable choices. Not how his story fell apart if you dissected it. "He has a thing for you."

She kept her focus out the window and off him. "I know."

That was news to Shane. "You do? Since when? I swear you denied it when I suggested it earlier."

She turned and shot him a don't-be-dumb look. "He all but told me to dump you because you're all wrong for me."

And now Shane had other reasons to hate the guy. "Not happening."

"I wouldn't." She smiled. "Because you're the perfect bodyguard."

That response didn't sit right with him. They'd had sex. He'd held her and kissed her. They spent time together and… Shane cut off his thoughts.

He'd been the one insisting they keep their relationship on a friendship level and now he was
getting all wrapped up over another man wanting her. Talk about sending mixed messages. Not
his style at all, but when it came to her, his feelings and common sense, and what he should do
versus what he wanted to do, got all tangled up.

"I don't trust him." Shane offered the explanation without fanfare.

"He performs an important service."

Shane wasn't as convinced. Yes, the site exposed men who deserved to be exposed, but
he couldn't help thinking Tyler had a hidden
agenda. Of course, every man associated with
the site struck him that way. Maybe his paranoia
was running on high.

"You don't think he's a little too good to be
true?" That was as far as he'd go…for now.

"You don't trust anyone."

She wasn't wrong. "I trust you."

"Because you like me, even though you fight
it." Makena's hand balled into a fist against the
door. "I hate this part of the drive."

Shane focused on the road and the narrow
bridge ahead instead of her throwaway comment. The span skimmed over the water for half
a mile. He understood the concern. Sometimes
the sun's reflection bounced off the water and
blinded drivers. "I've driven it a million times."

"Your skills aren't what has me concerned. Death by drowning is the main thing on my mind." She seemed to brace her feet against the floor as she stared ahead.

Shane looked at her and did a double take. They'd driven to Tyler's house via a longer route from another part of the county, avoiding the bridge. "I can turn around."

She shook her head. "I'm fine."

She didn't look it. She'd been shot at and looked less fatigued. Shane decided right then that he would never understand her. "The death grip on the door gives you away."

"Just drive. The faster you go, the sooner this will be over."

He admired her spunk. That and about a hundred other things.

The tires crossed the bridge entry with a thump. With the low sides, they could see the open water. It flashed by on both sides, and cables scaled above them. A few other cars passed in the opposite direction, but the road stayed clear.

A quick look in his rearview mirror showed a vehicle coming up behind him. It moved too fast, which suggested a kid or a driver confused about the concept of defensive driving. Shane kept watch, stealing peeks.

Then the mood changed. The truck, big and black, lined up behind him, way too close. He took in the large grille on the truck and the tinted windows. He couldn't make out the driver, but this guy was playing games.

Shane glanced over at Makena. She hadn't picked up on the tension. She sat there, fiddling with the radio. His gaze shot to her seat belt.

The revving of the engine had his attention zipping back to the mirror. He tapped the brakes, trying to back the guy off. If this was innocent, he should get the hint, but Shane sensed this was deliberate. Someone wanted to make a point. A very dangerous one.

"Hold on." He knew that didn't mean much, but he said it anyway.

She looked at him, confusion written all over her face. "What?"

He couldn't hide the facts. She needed to be ready. "We have company."

She shifted in her seat and turned around as the truck tapped their bumper. The move sent her flying forward. "What is he doing?"

"Letting us know we're not wanted around here." When the truck drifted in again, Shane turned the wheel and swerved the car into the empty oncoming lane.

The truck surged, then fell back. This was a game of chicken played out in three-thousand-pound car and a massive seven-thousand-pound truck. Not exactly Shane's idea of a good afternoon, especially since the size advantage was not on his side.

He shifted in his seat, sitting up higher as he started weaving from one lane to the other. The move would steal some of his speed but make him a harder target to hit.

His luck held out and the oncoming lane stayed empty. Shane just had to get them across. He hit the gas, thinking to outrun the larger vehicle in a race. But the truck wasn't ready to give in. He shot forward and smacked into the car's tail end. The move had the vehicle bobbling and tires screeching.

Makena grabbed the dashboard with stiff arms. Shane shouted for her to get down just as the truck ran alongside the car. Not even, but Shane could see the truck's heavy front out of his peripheral vision. See the make and the dark metal. Then the truck slammed into them, crashing them into the guardrail and snapping their bodies forward as far as the seat belts would allow.

The crunch of metal against concrete. The deafening screech as the car scraped against the wall. Shane kept his white-knuckle grip on the steering wheel, forcing the wheels straight and willing the car to stay on the bridge. The water seemed to get closer. It could have splashed up over the side and he wouldn't have been surprised.

With another slam, the car teetered and the wheel shimmied under his hands. He felt the front give and Makena's side ram into the concrete. They bounced and the world spun around them. The tires squealed and the smell of burned rubber and gasoline filled the air.

He could hear Makena's screaming as the force of the blow had her bouncing around in her seat, even with the seat belt. Shane fought against the skid and struggled to hold on to control. His heartbeat hammered in his ears as the car's back end crashed into something. The hit jolted his body until his teeth rattled.

A car horn honked and the sounds of skidding ran through his head. The car bounced and rocked on its tires. It left the ground and he waited for them to flip. A crack echoed around him, and then the car shuddered to a halt.

When his breathing slowed and he focused again, steam swirled out from under the hood. His gaze shot to the other side of the car. Makena had been pushed up against the door and rubbed her head as she mumbled.

He wanted to undo his seat belt, but he didn't know where the truck had gone or if they were alone. Still, he needed to know. He reached over and touched her hair. "Baby, are you okay?"

She nodded and blinked a few times. When she finally looked up at him, tears stained her cheeks and her hands shook. "You kept us from going over the edge."

The car felt uneven and pieces of concrete and car parts littered the road. He wasn't sure part of the car didn't hang over the edge of the bridge. Just the thought of that had anxiety punching his gut. "Barely."

He looked up and saw two cars parked ahead of him. People poured out with terror on their faces. He glanced around and realized they'd spun around and now sat on the opposite side of the road, facing the wrong direction. A quick scan sent a pain shooting up his neck. Shane ignored it as he looked for the truck.

He undid the seat belt and reached for his gun. As soon as his hand touched it he dropped his arm again. The people surrounding the car were shouting about the police coming and asking Makena if they were okay.

Friendlies, not hostiles. Someone might have seen something, could possibly identify the driver of the truck. Shane vowed to ask all those important questions once the ache in his side eased. He leaned his head against the seat and said a quick thank-you to the universe for keeping them from going over the edge. He knew how to escape a flooding car, but that didn't mean he wanted to practice the skill.

His head rolled on the headrest and he looked at Makena. "We should have gone the long way."

She reached over and took his hand. "Next time."

He'd spent his entire life thinking he didn't have an ounce of luck. Anything that could go wrong did. He'd had to earn all he possessed the hard way. But he looked at her, felt her warm hand in his and decided he might be lucky after all.

Chapter Fourteen

Cam grabbed two bottles of water out of the refrigerator and handed one each to Makena and Shane along with pain pills. "You two need to work on the concept of date night."

"We like adventure." Makena appreciated Cam's attempts to lessen the tension. Not that it worked. To be fair, an entire comedy team working round the clock couldn't restore a sense of calm at this moment.

She'd been a shaking mess at the crash site a few hours ago. It had taken two people to shoehorn her out of the car. The slam into the sidewall had caved it in. When the fresh air hit her, she'd thought her control would come whizzing back. Then she'd seen the black skid marks along the bridge walls and realized how close they'd come to being trapped in an underwater grave. It was a miracle she hadn't thrown up her lunch.

Connor and Cam buzzed around the safe house. They'd come with medical supplies. Connor insisted they visit some doctor she'd never heard of. Shane refused. She figured she'd go if he did. And truth was, he'd sustained the most injuries. She'd gotten thrown around and her insides jumbled, but except for the knock to her head and a sore elbow, she was okay. She'd be a bruise from head to toe tomorrow, but now stiffness was the main issue.

From Shane's scowl she guessed he wasn't happy about his injuries. "This isn't funny."

Nothing about the last week rose to the level of funny, but if she didn't laugh she might cry, and she could not tolerate the idea of curling up in the corner. She glanced over at Connor. He hovered over his laptop. Was on his phone. Asked question after question. Seemed like overkill to her.

"His neck hurts," she said, referring to Shane.

"I'm fine."

"He will be." Connor nodded in her direction. "What about you?"

"Everything aches. I should be one throbbing pain by tomorrow morning."

Cam laughed. "Sounds like fun."

"We need to focus." Shane got off the barstool, probably too fast, because he grimaced the second he moved. "This last attack went too far."

"Getting hit by a car is worse than being shot at?" Not in her book. It all mashed together, making every hour dreary. She watched Shane pace around the small space in front of the stove and realized there had been a few nonawful hours.

Shane scowled at her. "I'm serious."

So was she, but she didn't belabor the point. "Do you think we were followed from Tyler's house? If so, we should let him know."

Silence greeted her question. She'd expected more. A noise of some type. Agreement, maybe. Sure, they didn't know Tyler and Shane clearly didn't like him, but they protected. That was what the Corcoran Team did. They rushed in when others ran away. They didn't leave people behind or put them in harm's way.

Finally Cam spoke up. "Know what?"

"That the people launching these attacks know where he lives." It seemed simple enough to her. Tyler could walk into a trap or be the newest victim of a shooting.

They all looked at each other this time. Men frowning and acting confused—not her favorite thing and certainly not expected.

"Don't we already know that?" Connor shifted in his chair, leaning back as he delivered the question with measured words. "He claims someone broke into his house. You saw the aftermath."

She caught the doubt. Connor's tone never changed, only his word choice. The fact that neither Cam nor Shane jumped in to correct him couldn't be good. "Claims?"

Shane started to shake his head, then winced. "Let this topic go."

She sensed he was talking to Connor, but she didn't care. "I want to know what you guys are thinking."

"You don't," Shane said without giving her eye contact.

She sure did now. Inhaling as much air as possible, she tried to calm her flaring nerves and concentrate. "I have been shot at and almost drowned. The least you guys can do is not treat me like a little kid. I'm in this, so tell me."

Shane glanced at Connor, who nodded. It took another few seconds of silence for Shane to start talking. "His military record doesn't match the story he tells. Nothing he says makes sense."

She sat down hard on the barstool next to Cam. "What?"

"We've been checking into the past of everyone on the website and all the files Tyler turned over." Connor turned his laptop around to face her. "On the surface, Tyler is clean. On the surface, Jeff is dangerous and Frank is contrite."

Cam took over. "The men you're researching, that the site is researching, are mostly frauds. A few are clean. They embellish their records but nothing so extreme that it's worth calling them out and humiliating them."

She knew most of that, or had guessed it. But the phrase *on the surface* clued her in to bigger trouble. "But?"

"The man who came to your house and started all of this was on the loop with Jeff." Shane exhaled. "In other words, all of these men are connected."

They clearly thought they were saying something, but she could not follow what. "Didn't we know that?"

"Many claim not to know each other." Shane stopped as if weighing how much to say and how to say it. "They don't live near each other or have any public contacts, but there are contacts. Behind the scenes and not through the usual channels, like emails and phone calls."

"So this is some big conspiracy to wipe out the website." She could believe that. Push bad men hard enough and they shoved back. Some of the men who had been uncovered didn't have much left to lose. Going out by taking down the people who unveiled their lies would not be a surprise.

"Normally I would say yes, but there's more than that." Connor glanced at Shane.

He filled in the blank. "Tyler doesn't appear to be who he claims to be."

Anger rose inside her and she clamped it down. Her inclination was to rush to Tyler's defense, get indignant on his behalf. He'd never been anything but good to her. But she looked around and saw the faces of men who cared about her and her brother. Men who wouldn't lie. Men who clearly knew more than she did. "Explain that."

"The suspicions are in pieces. All circumstantial." Connor flipped the computer back to face him. "We can't prove anything."

"Yet," Cam added.

"These guys are passing information back and forth and hiding it. When you peel the layers away, Tyler's past looks more like the men he hunts than the people he purports to respect." Shane visibly swallowed. "I don't want you alone with him."

No matter what she did, grab on to the counter or blink, she could not stop the spinning in her head. The facts swirled. Every word he said ran through her mind and she tried to grab on and analyze each one. She didn't understand why Tyler would lie or how any of this could be true, but Shane's stern expression told her it was.

Tyler was guilty of something, maybe just coloring the truth. She didn't know, but the team would find out, and she would have to deal with the fallout.

"I hate being lied to." That qualified as an understatement.

Shane walked over to her. There, in front of his friends and coworkers, he wrapped his arms around her. "We'll find out that truth."

And she knew he would.

SHANE PUSHED INSIDE her as his muscles trembled and his breath punched out of his lungs. The thin legs of the bed shook and the springs rattled. He ignored every noise except the soft growl coming from the back of Makena's throat. He loved that sound.

Shifting his weight, he plunged again, in and out, slow and steady, until she grabbed on to his shoulders and tugged him closer. "Shane, now."

"I want it to last." He didn't realize he'd said the words out loud until they pulsed in his ears.

"I need to…" She threw her head back. "Please."

Her shoulders rose off the bed and her ankles dug into the back of his thighs. He pressed her into the mattress as she wrapped her body around his. Friction had their bodies rubbing together, ratcheting up the need flowing through him.

It had been this way from the first time. All

wild heat and pounding satisfaction. From her soft skin to every impressive curve, he could not get enough. For the first time in his life he wanted to crawl into bed with her and stay there. Forget work and responsibilities. Forget his past and every wrong turn he'd ever taken.

Her fingernails dug into his shoulders. "I can't hold back."

"Don't."

Before he even got the word out, her hips started bucking. Heavy breaths rocked her body as her lips skimmed over his chin. Energy spooled off her and wove its way around him. She clung to him, pressing her legs tighter against him. The tightness, the clenching, watching the orgasm rip through her, all combined to set him off. He wanted to wait, savor each pulse inside her, but his body had other ideas.

The tightness that had been building inside him let go. His muscles stiffened the second before they released. Unable to hold his sore neck up for one more second, he let his head drop. Buried his face in her shoulder and breathed in as the orgasm overtook him.

When his hips stopped moving, he collapsed, careful not to drop his full weight on top of her. Lifting off and out of her qualified as the sweetest torture, but then he was next to her with his arm wrapped around her shoulder and her body curled up against his side.

He dropped an arm over his face and closed his eyes. "That should not be so good." Nothing should feel that good.

She laughed and the sound vibrated against his skin. "Because I'm Holt's sister?"

Shane lifted his arm and stared down into her flushed face. "Because much more of that and I'll need a hospital."

"Challenge accepted." She leaned her head against his chest again.

This he could handle. The hot during and quiet after. He'd never really experienced the combination before. He loved feeling frenetic and out of control, but this, the part where he combed his fingers through her hair and drifted off to sleep, was new.

He never talked about this, but with her the temptation proved stronger than his will to put it all behind him. "Losing my marriage doubled me over."

She stiffened against him. "Do you miss her?"

"That's not what I mean." He didn't know how to explain and worried that even if he managed to put the right words together he might still sound like a jerk. "I liked the *idea* of being married."

She lifted her head and rested her chin on her hand. "I don't get it."

"Marriage meant family and security. It meant I managed to accomplish something." But he couldn't hold it together. "But I failed, and it knocked me off stride. I kept thinking that the divorce said something about who I was."

"You married the wrong person. That's all." She pressed her other palm against his chest. "You guys both wanted an out, but that's not enough. Marriage as escape can only go so far if there's nothing fundamental holding it up."

"You can't deny that the danger of my job is a huge stumbling block to anything long term and meaningful."

She nodded. "You better tell Connor and his wife. Talk to all the other guys on the team and explain that the love they feel now means nothing and that they should run."

"Okay, I get—"

"And then call my brother and tell him to leave Lindsey on the West Coast." Makena made a face. "He shouldn't waste his time building a life with her."

She made it sound so easy. So did the guys on the team. You fell, you accepted it and you tried to minimize the risks. It helped if you found a woman strong enough and determined enough to stand up and face the danger on her own terms.

"You should have been a lawyer." Because she made it all sound possible.

"I'm happy right here." She kissed his chest. "With you."

"I'm sorry you heard about the Tyler suspicions like that, with Cam and Connor standing right there." He rubbed a thumb over her forehead, then down her nose to her mouth. "I wanted to give you that information in pieces."

"I'm pretty tough, you know." She raked her nails over his nipple, lightly but enough to get the nerves underneath jumping.

He flattened her hand under his. "Toughest woman I know."

"That's probably an overstatement."

"Not at all." He shook his head. "The woman I've been watching has handled every awful thing thrown her way and kept standing. She's overcome her fear and stood up to Jeff, who is a guy no woman should have to deal with."

"We should call Holt."

Shane hadn't been expecting that conversation change. "Really?"

"If I can handle gunmen, I can handle an overprotective brother with a list of questions to ask."

"You're tougher than I am." Shane dreaded Holt's reaction. They knew so much about each other. Shane couldn't hide or smooth over anything. Holt would know exactly what kind of man wanted his sister, and Shane did not see that as a good thing. "But you're right. It's time."

"You're going to admit we've been sharing a bed?" She whistled. "Brave man."

"I think the word *dating* sounds less likely to get me killed." But not by much. Holt had made it clear Makena was off-limits. If Shane wanted to bumble around, sleep with other women and never get serious, Holt was fine with that, but Makena could not be another number.

She wasn't.

Her eyes widened. "Is that what we're doing?"

Good question. He honestly didn't know. "We can use whatever word you want. I just know I don't want it to end."

He'd finally said it. Admitted it to himself and to her. The walls didn't crumble and the earth didn't open up and swallow him. He'd survived the truth, that being a lone wolf grew exhausting as the days passed, and with her he wanted more.

She moved up his body until her lips hovered over his. "Good, because we're not over."

The words shot through him. Instead of running and panicking, he settled in and enjoyed. "I was hoping you'd say that."

Her fingers slipped into his hair. "Why don't you show me how grateful you are?"

"Done."

Chapter Fifteen

He couldn't do this one more minute.

Frank shut the cover to his laptop and leaned back in his chair. He'd been investigating every avenue, trying to figure out who had blackmailed him and thought they owned his every move. He'd followed instructions, thinking each new order would be the last. But the assignments bombarded him. He read discussions on the loop and picked out secret messages in every one. He had no idea if he'd grown paranoid or if his life really was closing in on him from every direction.

But he couldn't keep doing this. Every day he clicked on a news link, worrying some action he'd put in motion had ended in death. He'd made so many wrong turns, but he could not tolerate the idea of having more blood on his hands.

That meant coming clean. Taking the venom out of the blackmail and telling one last secret. He'd already been chastised and ignored. What else could happen? Begging Tyler to take his name off the site hadn't worked. Telling his blackmailer one assignment after another would be his last didn't threaten anyone.

The address. The license-plate number. The police contacts. Information on this Shane guy. Frank had done it all, and he was done. Long done.

He picked up his phone and dialed the number. In a half hour it would all be over.

"FRANK WANTS TO see us." Makena almost hated to utter the words. She didn't look up because she could only imagine the scowl on Shane's face.

When he didn't say anything and the silence continued, she glanced across to the other side of the couch. He'd been crouched over the laptop a second ago. Now he sat back and stared at her with a blank expression.

That couldn't be good.

She tried again. It actually didn't matter if he wanted to be convinced or not; they were going. "He sounds desperate."

"Did you talk with him?" Still no readable expression. Just the question.

She had her legs stretched out until her feet touched the side of his leg. She pointed her toes and pushed against him. "He texted."

"How does one sound desperate in a text?" Shane's hand went to her leg.

She didn't know if he even realized he rubbed a hand over her calf as he spoke. The gesture was so comforting. Sprawling on the couch as the rain hammered the roof felt normal and right. "My point is he asked that we meet him immediately."

His hand kept soothing and caressing. "We?"

The heat from his hand seeped through her jeans and touched her skin. She knew that probably grew out of her imagination, but she felt it. She also wondered why he thought she wanted to tackle anything on her own. "Of course."

Shane smiled then. "I like that."

"As if I'd be dumb enough to go into a meeting with any of these guys right now without firepower." She said it as a joke, but it kind of wasn't.

"So romantic." Shane stood up and reached down to her. "Let's go."

"That's it?" She stared at his hand, then looked at his face. His quick agreement minus a lecture stunned her. The guy thrived on lectures. "No arguments about the danger or…I don't know, anything?"

"You mean the part where this is likely a setup to get us both killed." His wiggled his fingers.

She grabbed on and let him lift her to her feet. "I wasn't going to put it that way."

"I'll call Cam and Connor on the way. They can provide backup and be our eyes."

"You didn't ask where we were meeting."

He dropped a quick kiss on her mouth before stepping around the couch on the way to pick up the keys to the loaner car Connor had gotten for him. "Somewhere dangerous and hard to guard, I'm assuming."

"Aren't you hysterical today?" More like light-hearted and calm. The thrum of tension that normally followed him had disappeared. He came off as relaxed yet just as determined as ever.

She had no idea what to make of the change or why it had happened. She half expected him to pretend to bring her along and then dump her off at one of the team members' houses for safekeeping while he rushed into danger. That was the guy she knew.

"Don't let the sarcasm fool you." He picked up his gun. Then a knife.

That was more like it. "This isn't a kinder, gentler Shane?"

"No such thing."

THEY ARRIVED AT the meeting place a half hour later. Not the park and not the diner. Not even the bridge where they'd almost died. They walked up to the marina that sat just a few miles from her house, which she hadn't been back to since the original shooting. Being this close to the scene where it had all started had something jumping around in her stomach. Nerves or panic... something.

She punched in the code Frank had given her and opened the gate to the docks. Shane followed without saying a word. He was armed and ready, and that was all that mattered. But as they made their way down the incline, she did see Shane's point. There were so many places to hide. So many ways to get lost in a maze of docks and ships, and not come out again.

She blew out long breaths as she struggled to maintain some sense of control. Her heartbeat ran off at a gallop and her chest ached from the force of it. She'd get through this. She had to. She had so much to live for, so much hope for the future for the first time in so long. She wouldn't give that up for a website or Jeff or Frank or anyone else.

The water lapped and metal clanked against metal as the boats bobbed in the water. No one was around. She knew Connor played some role in that. Rain or not, people should be milling around. The mist chilled her skin, but the total quiet was what had her ready to jump on top of Shane and demand he take her out of there.

They reached a T and Shane pointed to the right. "This way."

She looked down, mentally reading off the numbers as they passed each one. They needed 280. Of course it wasn't right near the front where the buildings sat. No, she walked beside Shane as the distance between them and land grew.

One final turn and they reached the point farthest away from the opening gate. Just a few more…something made her look up. Probably a hint in the way Shane carried his body or a shift in the breeze. It didn't matter why, but she saw Frank in front of her. Or a version of him. This Frank was disheveled and jerky in panic. He moved around, his gaze touring the distance as he stood there.

"What do you want?" Shane asked without any inflection in his voice. The wind whipped around him and the rain kicked up, but he didn't show any signs of being uncomfortable. He was in his element and in control.

Frank nodded toward the boat in the slip next to him. "We need to go inside."

Makena looked at the hull. The boat was small, and having any kind of conversation likely meant crawling under and into a space they couldn't see right now. Shane had been right about this, too. It was a setup and one they might not survive if they weren't careful. Sure, Connor lurked out there somewhere and Cam was submerged in the water, ready to come up firing. But one mistake, one second too late, and this could be the last shooting in this case.

She thought about her brother and how many good things lay ahead for him. Her mind wandered over all the mistakes and focused on the good times. On the bright moments of the past few days. She glanced at Shane and took in his strength and energy and realized loving him had switched from a desperate state to a happy one.

"There's no way we're getting on that boat." Shane widened his stance. "So talk."

Frank shook his head. "You're not in charge here."

"This says I am." Shane lifted his hand and flashed his gun. Didn't wave it around or make a big show. Just leveled the playing field with one small gesture.

But she needed to avoid whatever harsh thing came next. She also wanted to know why he wanted them here so badly. "Okay, enough." She glared at the man she once believed had turned a corner to a new life. "You called us, Frank."

Whether it was whatever he saw on her face or the gun, something got him talking. He slipped to the side, getting closer to the boat, but he didn't run as he talked. "There's a group. They've banded together to come after you."

The loop. The men who sat around complaining about getting caught. She hated them even more now. "Right."

"How do you know?" Shane asked in a deceptively soft voice.

Frank took another step back. One more and his foot would slip into the small space between the dock and the boat, and he'd fall in the water. "I've been helping them."

Pain shot through her. She'd believed in him. Stood up for him. "So the 'new Frank' thing is a lie."

"It wasn't my fault." He rubbed his hands together as he shifted around. Every movement choreographed the frenzy taking off inside him.

Guilt could do that to a person. She refused to feel bad for him. Not again. She could not be fooled twice.

"You never get tired of saying that, do you?" Shane took a threatening step forward. "That thing where you shift the blame and pretend you're not at fault."

"I'm being blackmailed," Frank said.

That didn't make any sense. Before he'd been exposed, sure. He'd been a potential target for anyone looking to benefit from people's fake backgrounds. "Everyone knows your worst secret. What can—"

"No." Shane shook his head. "We don't, do we?"

The blows kept coming. Makena could barely find her breath. "What did you do?"

Frank waved his hands in front of him. The haze covering his gaze suggested a battle waged inside him. He tried to spit out a sentence a few times before getting it out. "I hid the secret."

She knew that. Everyone knew that. The whole point was that his story only worked so long as people didn't know the truth. "And?"

"You weren't the first person to figure it out."

The words sliced into her. They sounded so ominous, and he stopped giving eye contact. The guilt practically radiated off him.

She hated to ask, but she had to know. "Who did?"

"He's dead. That doesn't matter right now." Frank visibly shook. "The attack at your house, the one on the bridge, those were me. Well, I caused them by passing on information."

Shane no longer hid the gun. It was up, and the fury pulling at his mouth and carving deep lines into his forehead suggested he planned on using it, and soon. "I'm going to kill you."

Frank held up both hands. "I'm…no…I'm… trying to help."

The stuttering matched the rest of his affect. The jumpiness and darting gaze made her want to sit him down and tell him to write it all out. Once and for all, let him unburden himself and then see what happened next.

"Tell me everything you know and how you found out." Shane stood there as if daring Frank to say no.

After a brief moment of screeching silence, he nodded. "I got a contact a few days after I joined the loop."

So he had known about it for a long time and had been a participant. She'd never been moved to violence before the past few days. Now all she wanted to do was hit people until they told the truth.

"When?" Shane asked.

Frank's gaze shot to her, then back to Shane. "Months ago."

It took all her willpower not to lunge at him. So much pain and needless waste of life, and all because a bunch of men didn't like that their lies had been uncovered. The whole situation made her feel sick and achy.

She knew Connor and Cam were following along, listening through the device attached to

Shane's shirt. They were taking it all down and would investigate. They'd ferret out the truth and make Frank and the others pay. But right now, in this second, it didn't feel like enough vengeance.

Shane somehow kept it together and continued asking questions. "Who contacted you?"

"That's it, I'm not sure."

"Guess," Shane shot back before Frank could finish his comment.

"I think we both know."

"There are a lot of suspects."

"But only one guy in charge." Some of Frank's panic subsided, as if talking lifted some of his guilt. "I'm sure it's—"

His words cut off as his body collapsed in a heap. One minute he was standing, and the next his body turned boneless and fell down, knocking against the boat and slipping into the water.

"Get down." Shane called out the order as he slammed her against the dock with his body covering hers. He reached over and grabbed for Frank's arm, but his body was already sliding under the surface.

She lifted her arms off her head and tried to focus on the voices. The quiet of the night hadn't broken, but she heard yelling. Familiar voices. She leaned in and heard the yelling in Shane's ear. Then came the footsteps. Pounding down the dock. Shane spun around, putting his body in front of hers as he sat up and aimed.

Connor stopped in midrun. "It's me. Don't shoot."

"Get down." She tried to repeat Connor's order, but her voice barely rose above a whisper.

He must have heard, because he dropped, crawling the last few feet to where they sat, stunned. "Either of you hit?" Connor looked from Makena to Shane.

"What happened?" She still didn't know. She hadn't heard the bang she'd come to expect in a shooting…and how sick was it that she had any expectations?

The gentle thud of the water against the boats turned into whoosh. Cam popped up, fully outfitted with scuba gear. Next her brother would pop out somewhere.

Dizziness hit her then. She leaned against Shane, trying to absorb some of his strength. "I didn't hear the shot."

"Silencer," Connor and Cam said at the same time.

A new word for her to hate. "Convenient."

Connor frowned at her. "How so?"

Shane spoke up then. "That's exactly what the shooter wanted to do to Frank, silence him."

"It worked." Her stomach wouldn't stop flipping. Her insides were scrambled as if she rode a never-ending roller coaster.

Shane put a hand on her lower back. "We'll make sure it doesn't."

For some reason, in that second, she believed him.

Chapter Sixteen

Shane had grown tired of everyone associated with the website. Really fast. He'd been close enough to get hit with blood splatter when Frank got shot. Scrubbing it off didn't wipe the stain clean.

Good guy or bad guy didn't matter. Frank had been young and misguided and had carried a secret that would fell most halfway decent men. Cam had connected the dots in no time. A friend of Frank's had died in an alley after a long night of drinking. The person with him? Frank. The friend had expressed concerns about Frank's stories before he died, and those concerns had died with him.

Shane didn't know what had happened in that alley, but he'd bet an angry confrontation gone wildly off track. A fight that left one friend dead and the other in an alcoholic spiral and now in the morgue. Life had handed Frank one last wallop. Shane just wished Makena hadn't been there to see it.

At least her color had come back. She sat on the couch with her legs crossed in front of her, hugging a pillow to her chest. She listened to Connor and Cam tried to make sense of it all.

"There are long periods of time when none of the men in the group are logged in to any of their electronics," Cam explained.

She nodded and kept nodding, then asked, "What does that prove?"

"They likely have an alternative source of communicating and were using that at the time," Connor finished, then sat there across from her. No one said anything, not even her, and he started talking again as if he felt the need to break it all down and explain it. "You can see bursts of activity before an event, like the attack at your house, then sustained inactivity during the actual attack."

The pieces made sense to Shane. Sometimes the lack of information proved to be better evidence than something obvious. Since Frank had only provided a piece—and a small one at that, without much detail—they had to fit it all together. Connor said he had the entire team working on the problem.

Makena tightened her hold on the pillow.

"This is so much work. If only they used that power for good."

"Men like that never do." Shane had learned that the hard way long ago. He'd hoped his father would change, ease up and actually be there. Never happened. Some men couldn't change. Men like Jeff thought he didn't need to.

"It's more fun to cause trouble," Connor said. "Speaking of which, Holt is on the way home to check on the two of you."

"No surprise there." She eased her grip on the pillow and tucked it next to her. "So, does all this mean we owe Tyler an apology? Can we clear him?"

Shane wasn't ready to go there. He didn't trust anyone involved in this case, and that only worsened with each hour. "No."

She frowned at him. "You sound so sure."

Shane pretended that look was about wanting more information and not about her being tied to Tyler. Shane knew she didn't have romantic feelings for the guy, but if she possessed a sense of loyalty, that could trip her up and make investigating Tyler harder. "It looks as if he lied about his service record. We need to know why and at what cost."

"I don't get it. Why start the site if he had this big lie in his past?"

That part confused Shane, too. There were

possible explanations, but none of them sounded especially smart. "Maybe to throw the scent off, or to get to the investigations first and keep any taint away from him."

Shane's money was on one of those. Tyler might just have the bloated ego to think he could be the one to successfully hide his fake past.

"This is so ridiculous." Makena pressed her head back in the couch cushions and wiped a hand over her face. "I was just trying to help."

The tone got to Shane. He sat down next to her and pulled her hand down. "You didn't do anything wrong."

Cam nodded. "The work is good. It's scary that it's necessary, but it is."

"Tell that to all the dead men scattered wherever I walk." She slipped her fingers through his and held on tight.

He moved their joined hands to his lap. "To be fair, I killed most of them."

Cam's eyes widened. "That's how you comfort her?"

Shane never broke eye contact with her. He needed her to believe the way he did. "She's tough. She doesn't need to be coddled."

"Man, Shane." Connor groaned. "This is almost hard to watch."

"You're not very good at this," Cam added.

"You're both wrong." She lifted their hands to

her lips and kissed the back of his. "He knows just what to say."

Once again, they were on the same wavelength. People could think whatever they wanted. Maybe he should come up with the perfect line and serve it to her, but truth was, when it came to her he didn't need to embellish. Flowery words were unnecessary. He felt what he felt. It knocked into him, punched him in the gut and had him reeling. Rather than be scared, he welcomed the sensations this time.

"Are you sure he's good at this?" Cam asked. "Because, wow."

"I am not weak." The words rang out strong and loud. She said them as if the comment resonated with her, rose deep from her belly.

Connor scoffed. "Definitely not."

From their reactions it looked as if they all knew. The important thing was she finally got it.

Shane winked at her. "No, you're not."

She stood up without dropping his hand. "Then let's go find Jeff."

There was a topic sure to wipe out his good mood. With one last squeeze, Shane let go of her hand. "That guy is mine."

The smile that crossed her lips could only be described as blinding. "So long as you end this, you can have whatever you want."

He didn't care who heard or how much crap he took for this. "Sold."

JEFF TALKED BIG. Puffed out his chest and delivered a full blowhard recitation, complete with anecdotes about how he'd been wronged. When it came to annoying displays of minimal self-awareness, this ranked right up there.

The scene went on for almost fifteen minutes. Jeff sat at the picnic table in the park that had served as the site of one of the many shootings during the past week. Shane and Makena sat across from him. She had to listen to how he'd been set up and how the charges had been blown out of proportion. She waited for him to spin out the oldie about how he'd worked in covert ops, so no one could know the truth.

Somehow he refrained, but she sensed he had that explanation in his arsenal. He just hadn't whipped it out yet.

When he finally started to wind down, Shane leaned in and stared at him. "You almost done?"

"You asked." Jeff looked back and forth between them with his gaze hesitating on her for an extra beat.

Just long enough for her to start shifting in her seat. The guy ticked her off. Every word he uttered sent her temperature spiking. The way he made himself the victim and tried to sell his hours logged on the gun range as proof his military story was true. His explanation was a convoluted mess, and she doubted she could hear much more.

"Tell me about the loop." Shane held a pen and turned it end over end on the table.

"What?" But Jeff's tone had changed. Just a hint and only for a second, but anyone listening for it would have picked it up. And everyone was listening in.

"You are the leader of a band of misfits who lied about being in the military and being heroes, and now get together to whine." Shane laid it on thick.

She almost cheered. Jeff didn't fear her but he might fear Shane. Or he would if he was smart.

Jeff didn't take the insults well. His skin flushed red and a vein in his forehead popped out. "You don't know what you're talking about."

"It's not as well hidden as you think." Shane passed the pen from one hand to the other. "My people found the loop and we're going over all the transcripts now."

"Who are *your people*?"

"You should be more worried about what we can do." Shane put the pen down with a click.

Something about the smooth move had Jeff's gaze shooting to the pen, then back to Shane's face. "You're bluffing."

"Frank Jay is dead." It hurt her to say the words. Hurt even more to realize he'd turned out to be less than the man she hoped he would be.

Jeff's mouth opened and closed, but that was all the emotion he showed to that announcement. "That group is made up of hardworking men who had their lives turned upside down by—"

She filled in the rest of the sentence. "Their own lies."

Jeff's balled his hands into fists. "She—"

"Discovered your lies, but you are still the liars, and when you get together to plan violence against other people, you are also criminals." Shane held up both hands. "It's simple math."

"Violence." For the first time Jeff's face fell. He stopped the chest puffing and all the other nonsense and sat there with a stunned, open-mouthed expression. "What are you talking about?"

For a second she bought it. Got sucked into the look and the stuttering tone. Then she remembered who he was and how well he could sell a story. "You celebrated me getting attacked."

"Someone talked about it." He hesitated between each word. "There are hard feelings, sure, but no one on the loop had anything to do with that."

Shane never took his focus off Jeff. It was as

if he was constantly assessing and analyzing. "The evidence suggests otherwise."

Jeff jumped to his feet. "The evidence is wrong."

The drama was back in full force and she was even less impressed this time than she had been during the first round. "Sit down."

"You can't tell me what to do." He muttered something under his breath. Sounded like a nasty name.

"Yeah, she can," Shane said.

Jeff slowly sank until his butt hit the bench again. "I'm being set up."

It was Shane's turn to swear under his breath. "Is that the only excuse you know how to say?"

"You don't understand." Jeff's gaze traveled between them. He threw in the gestures and facial expressions. Seemed determined to convince them of his innocence. "We blow off steam. We talk about how to put our lives back together, to find jobs. To figure out how to take down the website and erase the information that's been spread."

That didn't amount to gunfire, but it had the potential to blow up into that. People could talk in code or get the wrong idea. The dangers of groupthink were especially high when the group had a single sworn enemy. In this case, her. "So you know, nothing about that sounds innocent."

Jeff shifted in her direction. Spoke straight to her. "If something happens to you, the stories get told again. The spotlight will switch from you to us in a matter of minutes, and all the information on the website explodes all over our lives again."

She figured that probably was an accurate description of what would happen. She refused to feel guilty about that. "So?"

"Making you a martyr would make my life hell." Jeff glanced at Shane. "That's the reality. I need you alive and well, and preferably quiet."

"Or would it free you if she were gone?" Shane asked.

"You're wrong." Jeff's shoulders fell. It was as if the air rushed right out of him, deflating him. "Both of you."

With one final exhale, Jeff stood up. Slipped out from the bench and stood next to the table. He scooped his keys off the top and tucked them in his pocket. Didn't say another word as he turned around and started to walk away.

"Where are you going?" Shane asked in a voice that carried a cool chill.

Jeff still didn't turn around. "To find out who is setting me up. You'll see. I'll prove it to you."

She watched him go. The cocky walk was toned down, but the mess he left in his wake remained. "He's a bit too confident, don't you think?"

"He's had a lifetime of practice at lying."

Now, that was the truth. Somewhere along the line, lying had become Jeff's one true skill. The thought of that made her sad.

She rested her arm on the table and turned to face Shane. "So, now what?"

"Easy." He handed her the pen. Legal or not, the one with the microphone that taped every word. "We keep digging."

Chapter Seventeen

Tyler showed up the next day. Not at her boarded-up house or the picnic area or even at Corcoran headquarters. No, Tyler came to the safe house. Walked right up to the front porch and knocked.

Shane almost shot him through the door.

He'd tracked him as he came up the drive. Watched him ditch the car around a curve and not near the house. Normally it would have been out of the line of sight of the front door and almost impossible to see. The hidden security cameras helped fill in those shadows.

None of that changed the facts. Tyler shouldn't be here. He couldn't be here. The fact that he knew where to track them down, let alone that he'd left his house to travel to them, had Shane itching to fire his weapon. He fought the urge to grab the other man, drag him inside and slam him up against a wall.

He'd ducked questions and responsibility. For a man who spent his life exposing others, his secrets rose to the same level as many of the people he condemned. In Shane's mind, that made Tyler the worst sinner.

Shane let the guy get as far as the open entryway. Didn't invite him to sit down or have a drink. Kept him pinned by the door and within range of the gun tucked by Shane's side. He only got that far because Shane had had warning and could hide the documents and computers before Tyler walked in.

"Why are you here?" Shane asked even though he'd never believe the answer. Not now. Tyler had managed to wave a red flag that had Shane's back teeth grinding together.

Tyler's gaze stayed on Makena. "We need to talk about Jeff."

He could stare wherever he wanted. He likely thought he could win her over. That they still had a certain rapport. Truth was, she'd looked at the newest investigation documents an hour ago, and whatever loyalty she had to the man was waning.

Then there was the part where Shane didn't want Tyler talking to her. It wasn't a jealousy thing. More like Shane's control hovering right on the edge. He was looking for any excuse to take this guy out, and if Tyler said or did the wrong thing to Makena, he would do it.

"I'm more concerned with how you knew to

come here." With that move the target shifted to Tyler and stayed there.

"I have some tech skills and I—"

"No." Not a good enough answer. The Corcoran Team had the latest tech. The team didn't fool around when it came to staying undercover. If anyone even performed an internet search using any of their names, a message was transmitted back to headquarters. No way had Tyler just stumbled on some personal information while poking around. "This is not a house you find on a whim."

"I got the license plate off your car and followed you here." Tyler delivered the line as if he expected applause. But his own words kept tripping him up.

Shane wondered if Tyler knew how easy he made it to doubt him. "The same car that isn't actually in the driveway since I'm driving one I just borrowed."

Tyler shrugged. "Why does this matter?"

As subterfuge went, that response wasn't great. Shane let him get away with it anyway. "Because when people randomly show up where they should not be, I grow skeptical."

Tyler shook his head. "I get that you take your job seriously."

Shane ignored the condescension. He had a feeling he'd have to ignore a lot of annoying stuff if he wanted to make it through this conversation without having his head explode. "Which job?"

"As Makena's bodyguard."

She finally moved. Instead of taking on the bodyguard comment or anything else, she homed in on facts that brought the visit into question. "Tyler, you told me you never leave your house. You stick close and limit your contact with the outside world."

"You matter to me. After Frank…" Tyler held up a hand, gave a big show as if he couldn't talk and had to force the words out. "That was too awful."

Makena didn't back down. She tilted her head and kept rattling off the attacks against her. "Someone followed me, us, from your house, or it certainly seems that way."

"I heard about the bridge accident, and there's chatter online," Tyler said even though she hadn't specified which incident. "Jeff is feeling hunted and looking for revenge."

Interesting how he changed the discussion. Shifted the attention off him and onto Jeff. Made an allegation without actually saying anything negative.

Her eyes narrowed. "You think he'll hurt me?"

"He's on the edge and desperate." Tyler looked at Shane then. "You guys keep talking with him."

Shane guessed that was supposed to be some

kind of shot. It would take a lot more than that to knock him off task, and right now the task was to get as much information out of Tyler as he could before putting a bullet in him. "How do you know that?"

"I follow the chatter."

All of a sudden everyone knew about the supposedly private discussions on the loop. "But you didn't bother to tell Makena that the loop existed so that she could be prepared, too. She had to find out through Frank."

"I didn't take it seriously."

Shane really wanted to hit this guy. He had so many reasons—the way he looked at Makena, the fact that he put their safe house at risk and on general principle. "Do you take your position seriously?"

"What does that mean?"

"Your service record doesn't check out." Makena dropped the biggest bomb of all without flinching. The words came out and then she waited.

Tyler did not disappoint. His expression morphed from concern to disappointment to a touch of anger as Shane watched.

"You're reviewing my records?" Tyler glared at both of them this time. "You can't be serious."

"You were never in combat. You didn't serve in Iraq." There was no need to hold back now.

Shane wanted to spook the guy, get him to cough up some piece of intel that might make this entire case fall into place. Now he had doubts and gut feelings. Some evidence but not enough.

"I can see where you'd think that, but my files are confidential." Tyler's smile could only be described as smarmy. "You need specific access."

Shane was done playing with this guy. "I have it."

Some of the color drained from Tyler's face.

"Tyler, the facts and times don't line up. People you supposedly served with couldn't identify you." Makena delivered more of the information in a slightly less hostile tone.

Shane had no idea how she managed it. "The records don't show what you think they show."

Tyler shook his head. "You don't understand how this works."

"I've been researching for a year." A thread of anger moved into Makena's voice. "I think I do get it."

"And I'm retired army, so I know I do," Shane said. When all the life ran out of Tyler's face, Shane knew they had him spinning and worrying. "I have contacts. I work for people with endless contacts."

"I can bring you my file."

The last desperate gasp of the lying man. "Oh, I looked at it. All fake."

Tyler's mouth dropped open in mock outrage. "That is not true."

"I'm thinking you started the site to keep the upper hand. You got first crack at any research and could see if anyone was getting close to your lies." It was the only answer that made sense, even though Shane wasn't convinced it did.

"That's ridiculous. Makena, tell him." Tyler shot her a quick look. Then his gaze came back. His mouth fell even flatter. "You believe him?"

"You taught me to research. I researched your record." She shook her head. "It does not check out."

"This is him." Tyler backed up until his ankle hit the door. He kept pointing at Shane and stumbling as he rushed to say whatever was going on in his head. "He wants you all to himself."

She shrugged. "He has me."

If he hadn't loved her before, he would have right now. Shane decided to congratulate her later for that hit.

The outrage had Tyler sputtering. "I'm leaving."

Shane didn't argue. He'd be too busy packing and hauling Makena to another safe place to stay this afternoon to get sucked into Tyler's strangeness. "Don't you want to tell us why you came by for a visit?"

Tyler grabbed the doorknob. Wrapped his hands around it and held on. "You'll be sorry."

SHE NEEDED A BATH.

Today's meeting with Tyler had done her in. Makena used to like him, respect him. Now she could barely tolerate standing in the same room with him.

The breadth of his actions hit her. This wasn't a onetime thing or something that could be brushed aside, because it amounted to nothing. "He lied about all of it. Every last piece."

"Yeah, I think so, too." Shane exhaled as he looked out the window. Whatever he saw had his attention. She knew Tyler's leaving kicked off that celebration.

"I know that doesn't definitely make him a killer or the guy we're after, but it taints everything." She didn't believe anything Tyler said now and wasn't in the mood for excuses. They'd celebrated victories for the site, and now they all rang hollow.

"I'm sorry." Shane put an arm around her and pulled her close. "All indications are he was average at everything he tried. Not a stellar student. Not much of an athlete. Not very popular. The type who tried to buy friends using the trust money he got when his wealthy parents died in a plane crash." Shane whispered the words into her hair. "Pretending to be a hero might have been what he thought he needed to do to change his life."

"But he's such a loner. Lying about his life isn't getting him anything." She searched her memory but couldn't think of a single time he'd used his tales to soak up attention or win over friends.

Shane winced. "Maybe he thought it would get him you."

She couldn't even process that. Refused to think about it. "I can't believe I was so wrong. I thought I could read people."

Questioning this led her to question so many other things. She wondered if she saw things as she wanted them to be. Maybe she painted her entire life with one broad brush.

"Don't do that." Shane's voice stayed low and soothing. "Don't take on any more guilt."

It was possible she'd miscalculated about Tyler and put her faith in the wrong person. But she wasn't wrong about Shane. She refused to believe that was even possible. Her head rested against his heart, and his hand slipped into her hair. She craved this closeness with him and loved that he granted it to her so freely.

She listened for his heartbeat and relaxed into the gentle thumping sound. The higher-pitched beeping had her head whipping back. She looked up at him. "What's that?"

He frowned as he lifted his arm. "My watch."

The simple black band. All of the Corcoran Team members wore one. It was part of the uniform, to the extent that they had one of those. She'd never seen him not wearing it. The thing could perform miracles. It did so much more than tell time. It functioned as a camera and a computer, and it gave them the ability to tune in to each other at all times through some sort of internal comm.

But she'd never heard it make noise before. "That's an odd sound. Is it an alarm?"

He froze. "We need to get out of the house."

"What?" She pulled back, letting a breath of air separate their bodies as she tried to figure out what put the edge of frustration in his voice. "Why?"

"There's a bomb in here."

The comment didn't make any sense. "The watch?"

"The house, so move." He had her by the elbow. Got her almost to the front door before he stopped. "What did he touch?"

She had no idea what Shane was talking about. In the past few seconds he'd morphed from this solid male who held her to a guy talking in half sentences. She'd ask him why and try to get more information if she even had a clue what to ask. She didn't.

She tried anyway. "Shane, let's sit down and—"

"Do not move." He held a hand out to her to stay put as he stepped closer to the door.

He'd given her the exact opposite order a second ago. Before the tension had clogged the room to the point of suffocation.

He squatted down and stared up at the underside of the knob. "There you are."

It was as if she'd been thrown into a strange survival movie. She'd come to expect the unexpected and go with it, but this tested her resolve. She could handle these trials, but this one she did not understand.

She tried to grab him as he paced around the small area. "Could you slow down and explain?"

"Later." He walked through the house to the bedroom, tugging her behind him. "We need to get out."

They got the whole way to the bedroom before she built up enough strength to turn him around to face her. She caught his head in her hands just as he lifted the window and let the unusually cool air move in. "Shane, look at me."

He covered her hands with his. "Tyler planted a bomb."

The words sat there for a second. Then she

got moving. She wanted to race to the front door and run screaming out into the trees. But he had steered them in here and she had to think there was a reason. She helped him open the window. The next minute he was shoving her through it.

"Run and do not stop." He lifted her legs over the sill and helped drop her to the ground outside. They were on the ground floor and didn't need any acrobatics. "I need you to keep moving and not look back. No matter what you hear."

Her feet had just hit the ground when the bang exploded all around her. A wall of heat smacked into her, lifting her up and sending her flying backward. The noise blocked her ears and took her airborne. She finally hit the ground with a jolt, landing half on her butt and half on her elbow.

In her haze she couldn't think about anything but crawling. She took off, slithering across the ground, as unidentifiable charred pieces landed around her. She didn't totally understand what had happened, but she sensed she couldn't stop. If she did, something could hit her, and with debris all around and flames popping up everywhere she looked, she didn't want to take the chance. Her sole focus stayed on survival.

By the time she rolled over on her back and looked behind her, flames were licking up the walls of the house, and black smoke was billowing from every window. Fire rained down all around her. She scooted on her backside to put as much space between her and the inferno as possible.

Rocks and dirt dug into her palms, and the fire burned hot enough to scorch her cheeks. She kept backing up as her mind switched to one concern—Shane. She searched the landscape, looking for his shoulders. For a shape. For some sign of him.

He'd been right there with her. He'd climbed out…or had he? The memory replayed in her mind, and the horror struck her. He was still inside.

She scrambled to her knees. The hard ground bit into her skin, but she was too busy searching for an easy path back into the raging flame and inside the falling-down building to find him. He could not die. She would not allow it.

Her breath hiccupped in her chest and she choked back a sob. Despair threatened to swamp her, but she pushed the dread away. She had to believe. He was the strongest, most competent man she knew. If anyone could beat a fire, it would be him.

She tried to stand up, but her legs didn't hold her. She crumpled back down in a heap as every muscle turned to jelly. She'd turned boneless and the shock of what had just happened began to settle in. She rotated between hot and cold as she sat there, listening for the sirens and rocking back and forth.

He could not be dead. The words screamed through her head. She wanted with all her soul for them to be true.

A rumble of noise drew her attention. Fire was so loud as it consumed and destroyed. The sound of the flames rolling over everything in their path had taken on a human vibe. Smoke lifted into the sky and settled around her as she tried to figure out what to do next and how to get in there. Her mind went blank and her heart cracked in two at the idea of Shane not getting out.

Then the pity drifted away and determination moved into its place. She could not just sit there. He had to be alive and she had to find him. She looked around, spinning in a circle and adding to her dizziness. This time she had to get up. She balanced on her palms, then lifted herself. Her knees buckled, but she eventually stayed up.

She took two steps before holding an arm over her head to fend off the mix of smoke and heat. But she couldn't wait. She forced her legs to move. Slow and sure, she got closer, but not close enough to break in or for her frantic screams to be heard over the roar of the flames.

She stumbled and her ankle turned. Somehow she managed to stay on her feet. One more step and then a new round of confusion started. The whack to her back had her pitching forward. She put out her hands just in time to keep from landing on her face.

Her knee hit the ground first and then her hands. A shot of pain moved through her as she tried to figure out what had hit her. A piece of the house or something. The smoke made it hard to see much of anything and kept stealing her breath. With every inhale, she'd double over hacking.

She needed air to fight this fight. Rolling over to her back, she opened her eyes and tried to breathe in semifresh air. She saw something. A few blinks and it didn't disappear. There, off to her right, she spied jeans and a man's legs.

Her heart did a grateful flip. *Shane made it out!* Her gaze lifted and she saw that face. The wrong face. Tyler stood there, holding a gun.

"What are you…" It hurt to talk and she doubted he could hear her over the thunder of flames and crackling and falling debris.

He reached down and lifted her to her feet as if she weighed nothing. He brought his face in close to hers.

She tried to focus and listen to whatever he was saying. She picked out one sentence and her blood turned from burning to icy cold.

"This would have been easier if you'd chosen me."

Chapter Eighteen

The explosion dropped Shane to his knees. The ground shook beneath him, and the walls caved in over his head. He braced his body for the blows to come. The rafters would break and wood would tumble down on him.

But he'd gotten her out. He'd shoved her out the window and heard her scream and the explosion ripping through the small house. Cam and Connor would grab her. They'd find her wandering around and take her in. Shane refused to believe anything other than that. She hadn't been injured and wasn't stuck in harm's way.

With her safely tucked away in his mind, he concentrated on saving himself. He wasn't sure that was even possible. Smoke obscured his vision, and the fall had him doubting which way led to the outside and which led to the flames.

Heat pulsed all around him. He felt his clothing singe and the hot air tear through his throat and lungs. He covered his mouth and kept low, tried to remember all of his fire training. It had been a while and he was rusty, but he looked for light. For any sign of the world outside the burning walls.

Something smashed into his shoulder as he struggled to drop to his stomach so he could crawl. Pain seared his neck and he jerked. Saw a piece of burning wood fall to the floor. That had been on him, and he knew the amount of falling debris would only increase in the next few minutes. If he was going to crawl, he had to do it now.

His face hugged the floor as he fought for the last few breaths of untainted air. Every move hurt, but he kept going. Crawled in the direction where he thought he'd last seen Makena. Noise roared around him in a deafening cadence. He twice fell to the floor when the walls crumbled around him and threatened to flatten him.

He somehow kept going even though he felt as if his progress amounted only to inches. He couldn't draw in enough breath to focus. His strength waned as his last reserves of energy petered out on him.

He kept counting in his head. Concentrated on the image of her face and how good it would be to see her, touch her, again.

Something clamped around his waist and smashed him into the floor. He kicked out and struggled, trying to lift his arms and legs despite the fact that they suddenly seemed to weigh hundreds of pounds each. The battle got away from him. His ability to fight drained from him.

In his smoke-induced stupor he swore he saw Cam's face, filled with concern through the mask. Then his body floated. Shane couldn't explain it and feared he verged on passing out. Hallucinations and sliding into unconsciousness. If those happened together he sensed he'd die.

With one last kick of adrenaline he surged up, thinking to throw himself into the nearest wall. Instead he slammed into something that felt like a body. Arms wrapped around him and pulled. The smoke drifted over him, and then he broke free. He could see the ground and fire.

"Shane, talk to me." Connor's voice washed over him.

He chalked it up to one last strange vision. Connor wasn't exactly the last person Shane thought he'd see before he lost it. Connor held something. Then Shane inhaled and his senses cleared. A mask covered his mouth, and fresh air pumped through him, burning him. He had to throw the mask off to cough.

He doubled over as the painful hacking overtook every muscle. He felt as if he were being sliced and torn from the inside out.

The roughness in his throat made it difficult to

swallow. But he was alive. Connor stood in front of him with Cam off to the side, stripping out of a blanket that had been wrapped around him.

They'd gone in after him and yanked him out. Probably never even weighed the risks. Cam had performed the rescue, but Connor had likely choreographed it. Bottom line: without them, he'd be dead. Corcoran had saved him in every way possible, including here and now. The move humbled Shane and he was filled with gratitude, but there was one piece he needed to fit in with the rest. Her.

When he straightened again, he felt weak and exhausted, as if every last ounce of strength had been used up and expired. One thought kept going through his mind. "Where's Makena?"

Cam and Connor glanced at each other as the flames danced all around them. A gnawing sensation started in Shane's gut. A new burst of energy hit him and drowned out everything else.

"Connor, where is she?"

Cam stepped in next to him and they stood there like an impenetrable wall, blocking his view of anything else and his line to the fire. Anxiety welled inside Shane and he had to fight to keep from tearing down the burning structure with his bare hands.

Connor held up a hand. "We need you to stay calm."

"Where is she?" That was all he wanted to know. He could take another step, another breath, once he knew.

Connor's hand didn't fall. "Listen to me."

"Just show him." Cam stepped to the side and pointed. In the distance, on the other side of the wall of flames, a figure crouched down. Large and male. He lifted something...Shane blinked and tried to get his sore eyes to focus. Makena. Tyler had Makena.

He surged forward, intent on yelling and running. Strong hands held him back. Cam and Connor wrestled with Shane, dragging him to the ground as they covered his mouth and held on. His reduced strength was no match for their combined attack. He struggled to break free, shoving at them and landing more than one punch.

"We have to get her." The words echoed in his brain as desperation washed over him.

Cam held him from behind and Connor knelt in front. Their will pounded into Shane, but he tried to wave it off. There was no other play here. They needed to start shooting and not stop until Tyler dropped to the ground.

"We'll follow," Connor said in a tighter voice than usual.

Not good enough. Shane wanted her away from that guy. He'd walked right into the safe house and planted a bomb. Had done it like a pro. No sweating or panic. In Shane's mind that made the guy some sort of psychopath and put Makena in even bigger danger. "Now, we go now."

"We'd never make it in time thanks to the fire." Connor shook his head. "And we'd put her in the middle of a shootout."

"She'll lead us right to Tyler." Cam said the words right into Shane's ear.

"She is not a decoy. She can't...no." He looked from Connor to Cam. "Would you agree to this for Jana or Julia? No way. This is the same thing." Words tumbled out of him. "And if you don't care about how I feel, think about Holt. He'll kill us all for letting her be in danger for even one second longer than necessary."

They would fight for the women they loved, and so would Shane. Even if it meant knocking out two of his closest friends.

"She's going to be fine. I promise you." Connor sounded so sure, as if he believed every word he said and that by saying them he could make them true.

But Shane knew better. His mind started to clear, and the list of things that could go wrong piled up. "You don't know that. You can't possibly know that."

Connor stood up. "You don't have a choice."

Shane had never felt so desperate or helpless. "Connor, please."

Cam lifted Shane to his feet and stood with Connor. "Let's go."

It hurt to stand up. Hurt to breathe in. Shane vowed to suck it all up and take it if it meant saving her. "If this doesn't work…"

Connor handed Shane a gun. "It will."

TODAY HAD ROLLED out like a nightmare in her head, and it wasn't over yet.

Makena needed a hospital before the dizziness overtook her and she passed out. She also needed some word about Shane. Her insides felt shredded. Panic ran through her like air. Her mind kept zipping back to the moment of the explosion. She tried to remember pulling him out through the window with her, but feared that was wishful thinking. That it had never happened.

If she were anywhere else, if she had minutes to think, she might be able to put the pieces together in her head. Instead she sat at Tyler's kitchen table and played house. He walked around serving coffee, acting normal. Or some version of normal.

"Tyler, please listen to me." She tried to move her arm and bit back a scream when the bindings cut into her skin.

She couldn't move her legs or arms. She tried

to wiggle her hands behind her, get a little bit of give in the rope so she could slip a hand through, but they were so bound so tightly her fingers had started going numb.

He sat down across from her and opened his laptop. "We'll go to dinner soon, and then you should go to bed early."

He spoke as if this were their routine instead of some messed-up delusion in his head. He'd suffered some sort of break. No question. The anger he'd had back when Shane confronted him had disappeared. This Tyler acted as if they were locked in a twisted form of domestic tranquility.

She would have ached for him if she could conquer the terror buzzing in her head long enough to think about anything else. She didn't think he would hurt her, but she didn't know. This Tyler was not a man she knew. He'd been pushed to the edge and now he lived in a world she didn't understand. One that had fear crashing through her so hard that she had to fight back tears.

"Could I go to the bathroom?"

Tyler peeked up at her. Fury highlighted his features. One minute he looked ready to tuck her into bed and the next he looked as if he could kill her. This was one of those latter moments. "No."

She wanted to reason with him, bring him back to reality. She didn't even know if that sort of thing was possible. "You can untie me."

"So you can go to him?" Tyler snapped the laptop shut. "No."

Shane. She thought about him and sadness rolled over her. She had to fight back the tears and pain, and push through. "We can talk about this."

Tyler shook his head. "You gave me no choice."

Okay, she could handle this. "I did."

His gaze narrowed. "We had something and you threw it away."

She had to assume this was part of the delusion. A piece where he viewed whatever they'd had as more than a working relationship. "I didn't know how you felt. You never told me."

"You knew."

Some part of her sensed that she needed to keep him talking and prolong this as much as possible. It would take forever for the team to discover her missing. And if they were busy mourning Shane...no, no, no. She dragged her thoughts back from that abyss and kept pretending. "How could I?"

The legs of the chair scraped against the floor as he pushed it back and stood up. "That's not possible. I gave you more and more responsibility. I risked everything for you."

"Tell me how." She tried to lure him in while she spent every spare second visually searching the room for a weapon. "What did you do for me?"

"You researched cases that came so close to me. You almost wrecked all I built, but I forgave you." Tyler dumped out his freshly poured coffee in the sink. "I had it handled until that request came through the website. I got them all, but that one slipped through to you."

She remembered the day well. She'd been looking for a response to something else and had seen the request. Stumbled over it, really. "You were in DC doing research."

He smiled at her. "Just my luck."

"Why did that one matter so much?" The subject of the email inquiry had claimed to be Special Forces and a combat veteran. There was talk about sacrificing everything for his men and saving lives. The usual. Nothing exceptional that would have tipped her off or led her back to Tyler.

He shrugged. "We both borrowed the same life story."

The admission, so subtle and delivered without any emotion, left her breathless. He acted as if his deception didn't matter. She didn't know if that was the sickness talking or something evil. "You're saying...what are you saying?"

"The man you were to investigate told a story much like my own because we both knew a man named Roger Culp. We all grew up in the same small town."

The truth hit her then. "But only one of you actually went to war."

"He was a local hero." Tyler leaned back against the sink and glanced at one of the small monitors attached under the counter. "There was no reason I couldn't enjoy some of those accolades. Outside the town, of course."

The justifications sounded so familiar. She heard them every day from the men they listed on the site. That her own boss, the man who had started the project, was one of them hit her like a sharp kick to the stomach.

He nodded toward the monitor. "We have company."

She followed his gaze, hoping to see Shane ready to storm in, but Tyler didn't show any fear. From this distance she saw a fuzzy figure outlined in black and white hanging around the front door. A man, but not her man.

As if she'd willed him to do it, he lifted his head. Jeff. The man she'd grown to be more and more uncertain of as the attacks kicked up in intensity. He showed up without warning and his anger festered just under the surface. Now she knew why. He was Tyler's contact. Likely his way onto the loop, where he could watch and contain the information passed around.

"Your partner is here." In that moment, she hated them both.

Tyler's eyebrow lifted. "Not mine."

Not what she'd expected him to say at all. With his narcissism she'd waited for some sort of self-congratulations. She got something very different. "What do you mean?"

"Your failure to keep up makes me second-guess my faith in you." Tyler tucked his gun behind his back. "I'll invite him in."

He walked away, out of her line of vision. She tried to turn in the chair, but the rope dug into her and burned her skin. Moving her head from side to side, she tried to pick up some clue. She didn't hear any conversation, just footsteps.

Then Jeff appeared in front of her. His eyes were glazed over with fear and Tyler had a gun pointed at his head. The hold Tyler had on Jeff's arm didn't make any sense. If they were working together…she didn't get it.

"Jeff stopped by to say hello." Tyler smiled as he said the horrible words.

Jeff's gaze traveled around the room, over her. "You tied her to a chair."

"What did you think he would do?" After all the killing and all the attacks, this ending could not be a surprise. It wasn't to her. She'd seen it coming and tried to avoid it, but failed.

"I thought you were working." He let out a

startled gasp as Tyler threw him in a chair. "I wanted to talk."

Tyler used his free hand to wrap a rope around Jeff's chest. The movements proved awkward and ineffective, and he finally let the bindings drop to the floor unused. "You won't be alive that long anyway."

"What is going on?" Jeff sounded confused and lost, and both emotions were mirrored in his eyes.

For whatever reason—the fear, the panic— she believed him. "I found out Tyler lied. That he's one of you."

Jeff spun around and stared at the man looming over him. "You weren't in the military."

A crazed look of desperation lit Tyler's face. "Stop talking."

All she needed was a free hand, but she couldn't get one loose, so she kept the men talking, saying anything to avoid a bullet to her heart. "You didn't know?"

"I would have used it against him." Jeff shook his head. "I can't believe this. After all this time—"

"I said stop." Tyler shifted until he stood at the head of the table between them. He slipped a knife out of the block and pointed at one of them, and then the other. "Let me explain what's going to happen. Jeff, you are going to kill Makena in a horrible revenge-filled frenzy."

The color drained from Jeff's face as he tried to slide his chair away from Tyler. "I would never—"

Tyler linked his foot around the chair leg and dragged Jeff closer to the tip of the blade. "Makena, you're going to get one good stab in, and it'll wound poor Jeff here. But I'll deliver the final blow with the gun I keep for protection."

He'd clearly written the sick scene in his head. She'd failed to play her assigned role and now he gave her another one. "Like a hero."

He glared at her. "I am one."

"This will never work." Possible solutions ran through her head. She could crash her chair into him... She ran out after that.

"You had your chance. I wanted you to be my partner."

Her mind flashed on another scenario. One that would save Jeff, too. Her gaze flicked to him. "How did you get here?"

"I followed you."

She hoped that meant the Corcoran Team had as well. "I blamed you." The apology stuck in her throat. She couldn't get it out, not yet.

"He's a liar," Tyler said in a reasonable voice that carried over the mix of shuffling and chair moving happening on the floor.

She tried to pick up each sound and figure out what was happening. Jeff kept looking at her and then staring at Tyler's stomach. She wasn't sure what he wanted her to do, but she sensed she and Jeff were in this one together.

Jeff shot her one last intense stare. "No one will believe it. I'm not a killer."

"Unfortunately for you, I am." Tyler drew back the knife and stabbed it into Jeff's side.

She closed her eyes but not before seeing Jeff's pop open. He groaned and his body doubled over. Blood seeped through his white shirt. The room broke into chaos. The window on the side of the family room shattered and a male figure crashed inside. She turned her head to avoid the flying glass and saw the front door explode off its hinges.

Her eyes refused to focus, but she thought she heard Shane's voice. The yelling ran together with the banging. The last thing she saw was Tyler reaching for his gun, and then a weight knocked into her, sending her and the chair in a free fall to the floor.

Everything happened at once. A drumbeat thundered in her ears and she struggled to loosen her hands, but it was too late. Her body bounced and her head knocked against the hardwood. She heard gunshots as Jeff's heavy breathing echoed in her ears. Then she couldn't see or hear anything at all.

Chapter Nineteen

Shane had waited a beat too long. He'd wanted to race in the second Tyler shoved Jeff into the chair. Shane saw the two of them as partners. Sick men who deserved whatever happened next. The full wrath of the Corcoran Team could fall on them and Shane would not suffer one minute of regret. He valued life but not their lives.

Then he saw the blade and Tyler's gun and silently declared, "Go time."

The explosives tore the front door apart. Shredded it into sharp pieces and sent them flying. He didn't wait for the smoke to clear or the space to open, or even for Connor's signal. Shane ripped the debris out of his way, ignored the cuts to his hands and marched through the door.

He headed for Tyler and didn't stop. Not when he lifted the gun. Not when he fired at Jeff, who was a blur streaking across the table to cover

Makena. Not when Tyler adjusted his aim and the barrel pointed at the general chaos.

He could shoot anyone, looked ready to kill without spending one second thinking about it. He wasn't a man on the edge. He'd gone careening off it at rapid speed.

Shane didn't waste time trying to fix Tyler or reason with him. They'd passed that point long ago. To whatever extent he'd ever dealt in reason, he didn't now. Shane had no choice but to take him down.

He came in firing over the heads of Jeff and Makena, trying to get them to duck and stay down. He wanted to draw Tyler's fire and keep his mind off the bodies on the floor. In Tyler's obsessive state, anything could trigger him, and Shane didn't want to test him.

But Tyler didn't stick with the plan. He dropped down but kept shooting. He crawled toward Makena, and Shane increased his speed. Breaking every rule and ignoring protocol, he crossed right in front of Cam's line of fire, heedless of the danger and desperate only to get to her. All those hours of practice and drills faded into the background.

Connor swore and Cam yelled. Shane blocked it all. He had to, because she lay tucked and unmoving. Blood covered her, but he couldn't tell if it was hers or Jeff's, as they were piled on top of each other.

"Stay back." Tyler practically screamed the order as he reached for Makena's arm. He pulled, trying to drag her closer.

She shoved away from him. Jeff trapped her in place, leaving her vulnerable to Tyler's whims. The gun in Tyler's hand waved and bobbled. He pointed it in every direction, as if he'd forgotten he even held it.

The man was the ultimate wild card, out of control and raging. He started yelling about his life and all he'd lost. When he spied Shane, his intensity seemed to find a focus.

Perfect. That was exactly what Shane wanted. He made himself a target on purpose and planned to keep his body there for as long as possible. Let Connor and Cam get into position. Let Tyler make a mistake. Anything to take the attention away from Makena and give them all a chance at survival.

But Shane couldn't look at her for long. Her eyes were wild with fear as her mouth dropped open. The combined look of pain and fear killed him. So did the way she glanced around and silently begged Cam to do something when Shane didn't.

But he could. Rather than wait on the defensive, he grabbed a hold of the offensive. Shane held his hands up. "That's right. You want me."

Tyler scrambled to his knees. "You ruined everything."

Shane took a step back, luring Tyler away from the protection of the barricade of the tipped table and pile of fallen chairs. "I did. I went after her when I knew she was yours."

Makena gasped. "Shane, no."

For a second he worried she believed him, but the concern on her face suggested something else. She was smart and strong. She'd know this amounted to a plot meant to ensnare Tyler and drag him down.

When Tyler's gaze slipped back to her, Shane rushed to get it moving again. "I did it on purpose. I didn't want her, but I really didn't want you to have her." He shook his head and pretended to believe the foul words he spit out. "She was a game. I wanted to beat you."

Tyler lifted up a little higher. An inch more and his head would pop up in firing range. "She wanted me first."

Shane didn't even steal a look at her this time. To get through this, he needed to match Tyler's evil with some of his own. The anxiety pinging around inside him threatened to drop him to his knees, but he kept his attention steady. On Tyler and his gun, waiting for the perfect moment to take him out.

"She did want you. She was all in and talking about you. Thinking you were this hero doing all this amazing work." Shane forced the words out. "But I made her want me. Convincing her was tough, but I did it."

Tyler straightened then and Shane did not hesitate. He lowered his hand with exacting speed and fired. Gunshots rang out from three parts of the room and he knew Connor and Cam had taken the advantage, too.

But Shane didn't care about Tyler. Connor could handle him. Shane's mind went to the woman who held his heart. Ignoring the aches and pain and the way his bones creaked after all the abuse they'd endured, he slid across the floor and skidded to a stop beside her. He was vaguely aware of Connor dropping down to check Tyler's pulse and Cam rushing over to lift Jeff.

Shane only saw her.

He grabbed at the ropes binding her to the chair, trying to rip them apart with his bare hands. His strength alone might have done it, but Cam handed over a knife and Shane got busy cutting.

He had her loose in a few seconds and she flew into his arms. Her warmth seeped into him as he fell back against the floor on his butt. He had her cradled on his lap and he rocked back and forth. "I love you. God, I love you."

He could hear her crying and felt the wet tears against his neck. Sirens whirred to life around them, and car doors slammed shut just outside. Guns came up and people talked over each other. Jeff didn't move while Cam clamped a kitchen towel against his side and tried to talk with him.

Police burst through the door and Connor stopped them. He held up his hands and the yelling match started. All the noise faded into the background for Shane. He couldn't help them and didn't want to let go of her. In this moment he needed her. To hold her, to beg her forgiveness. Everything.

"I'm so sorry." He whispered the words over and over, into her hair, then against her forehead. He kissed the patches of skin he could see and brushed her hair out of the way to get to her mouth. He was about to ask her something when her mouth touched his.

She kissed him, deep and desperate. Her fingers clawed at his back and she drew him in closer. "I thought you were dead."

He had to lean down to hear her. "Are you hurt?"

She shook her head but didn't answer. For some reason he needed to hear her voice. "Baby, talk to me."

She looked up at him with tearstained cheeks. "It's Jeff's blood."

The reminder had Shane glancing over his shoulder. The man's eyes were open but glazed over.

"He saved me." A tremble made her voice vibrate.

"I saw." Shane had watched in shock as Jeff played the hero. He'd spent so much of his life lying about being one. In this instance, he'd acted like one, and Shane was humbled by the sacrifice.

"Is he—"

"Cam is working on him." An ambulance crew rushed in a second later.

The small room burst to life. First responders roamed around and Connor acted as traffic guard, moving people here and there. Being in control and running the room. Business as usual.

Makena grabbed a handful of Shane's shirt and brought his head back down to hers. "Get me out of here."

He could do that. He owed her that much. More, actually. Because of him she'd played the role of decoy. He'd put her in direct danger and then almost stepped in too late to save her. It was every nightmare brought to life. He'd stayed away to keep the ugliness of his work out of her life but ended up doing the exact opposite.

"I'm sorry." He said it because he had to. No other words would come out without a push.

Her hand trailed down his cheek. "You're my hero."

"I'm not, but you're alive and that's all that matters."

He stood up and lifted her into his arms. He knew she needed to see a doctor and get checked out. That would all happen, but he needed to hold her for a few seconds first.

She wrapped her arms around his neck and whispered into his neck, "I love you."

The guilt trapped inside him escaped. "You shouldn't."

He'd never meant the words more in his life.

If anyone had told Makena she'd be sitting at the hospital bedside of Jeff Horvath one day, she would have laughed. Maybe not even that. The idea was so ridiculous it didn't even sound like a joke.

She'd taken the position that Jeff had gotten what he deserved. Somewhere she'd forgotten that he was a human being and had tossed his feelings aside. He deserved most of what had happened to him, but his actions at Tyler's house showed that he could be redeemed. That there could be decency inside someone like him.

Once guilt stopped punching her, she'd appreciate the lesson.

Until then, here she was, watching the machinery work to keep him alive and get stronger. The room filled with beeps and strange sounds. Something clicked and an automatic blood-pressure monitor spun to life and checked him every few minutes. He had oxygen and tubes connected to him.

He hadn't opened his eyes, but the doctor said he'd survived the worst and was improving. She had no idea how anyone could tell.

She leaned back and continued to stare, willing him to get better and hoping he had the strength to do so. She did it for him and for her. Concentrating on Jeff helped her to forget Shane's last words to her.

You shouldn't.

After everything, all the pain and death, the terror and anxiety, he held on to his lone-wolf stance. In her horror-induced stupor, she'd thought she heard him utter the words she longed to hear. She'd told him she loved him, but he'd said it first…or had he? Those moments blurred together in her mind with Tyler's manic tone and Jeff's death rattle as the knife slipped inside him. Thinking about it had her eyes popping open.

"How is he?" Connor asked as he stepped into the room with Shane behind him.

"Better." But she barely heard the question.

Her gaze traveled over Shane. He had a bandage on his arm and neck, and one arm hugged his ribs. Connor had insisted they all take a trip to the hospital. She'd long ago been released. Shane had had to stay overnight and had slept through it all as she switched back and forth from his bedside to Jeff's.

Shane frowned. "That's a miracle."

It all was. Makena couldn't believe any of it. If she tried to explain it—and she had during a telephone call with Holt, who was ripping apart airports on his flights across the country to get to her—it all sounded so fantastical and unrealistic.

So did Jeff's sacrifice. "How could a guy who would lie about who he was step up like that when to do so risked his own life?"

Nothing about what Jeff had done and the choice he'd made fit with the other things she knew about him. He'd spent so much time pretending to be a hero when he had had the instinct for decency inside him all along.

Connor crossed his arms in front of him. "I like to think a lot of people would do the right thing if confronted with the opportunity."

Shane scoffed as he came over to stand beside her chair. "I think Connor is naive."

She kind of agreed. "I owe him."

"Connor repaid him." Shane's hand fell to her shoulder and squeezed.

The touch warmed all the chilled places inside her. She wanted to grab on to his hand and not let go. But now wasn't the time or the place.

Her gaze switched from Shane to Connor. "What did you do?"

"There will be a feature in the news about Jeff, touching a bit on his past for perspective but talking about how he turned his life around and saved you and other people during a wild shootout in a house."

"Connor left out the parts about Jeff stalking you," Shane added.

Connor shrugged. "It didn't fit with the rest of the story."

She gave in and touched her fingers to Shane's. "I'm sort of happy he did stalk me that last time."

He glanced down at her and winked. "Me, too."

With one last look at Jeff, Connor headed for the door. "I'm going to leave you two—"

"No." Shane snapped out the answer before Connor took his next step. Before she could agree.

She dropped her hand to her lap. "No?"

"I need to head out." Shane didn't make eye contact as he spoke. He glanced around as he moved away from her.

After spending so much of his life putting an emotional wall between them, this time he added a physical one. He was running away from her in every way she could imagine, both physically and emotionally. Even Connor stared at him with narrowed eyes as if trying to read his mood.

"Fine." That was all she could muster.

Shane hesitated as he watched her. "I'll call you."

Yeah, she wouldn't sit by the phone and wait for that call. In fact, she was done waiting for Shane at all. If he couldn't see that he could abandon his past and his fears, and be happy with her, she'd give up. They'd been in this highly stressful situation and managed to survive not by staying away from each other but by finally being together.

That left only one thing for her to say. "Goodbye, Shane."

And this time she meant it.

Chapter Twenty

The next day Shane waited outside the hospital for Makena to come out. He stood in the parking lot, leaning against her car. She'd been keeping vigil by Jeff's bedside since the ambulance crew brought him in. She'd called the Corcoran headquarters to let them know Jeff was going to be okay. She'd talked about going to Holt's house to wait for him to get in after a series of canceled flights delayed him.

Shane wanted to see her before Holt did. Wanted to see her...period.

Footsteps sounded beside him, but Shane didn't flinch. He'd seen Connor park nearby and head for him. He'd likely come over to give Makena a break at Jeff's bedside. A decent thing to do. Shane had never thought of it. He'd left her yesterday and stayed away because there was something he needed to do before he talked with her.

Connor took up position beside Shane and

stared at the front door of the hospital. "If Holt were here, he'd tell you to stop moping and go get your woman."

Shane turned slightly to face his boss. "What?"

"This, the doubt and guilt." Connor held out a hand in front of Shane. "I get it. Believe me. I almost lost Jana because I was so worried about *losing Jana*."

Shane had listened to many lectures from Connor during their time at Corcoran. The guy liked to talk and wanted things to be done his way. Shane appreciated the way Connor ran the business and the team. He had no complaints. Except for these talks that didn't make a lot of sense in or out of context.

"Clue me in on what you're talking about." His mind kept zipping back to Makena and all the things he needed to say to her. Talking with Connor just wasn't a priority, no matter how much Shane liked the guy.

Connor sighed. "Man, you're stubborn."

He'd been hearing that his whole life. Since Shane agreed, he didn't bother to deny it. "That's not news."

"I know you're invested in the whole bachelor thing."

Was. Before Makena. Before being with her and realizing he didn't want to be without her. "I am?"

"You're not?" Connor wasn't one to miss a clue. He didn't this time, either. "Are you saying—"

"I love her." The words that had once stuck in his throat now freed him. Shane said them and his whole world shifted into position. The failed marriage was behind him. Makena was his future.

Connor laughed. "I know."

"You could have told me." But Shane knew that wasn't fair. Each of the team members had talked about the difference between life on his own and life with a woman who meant everything. They'd tried to sell him on getting involved again and taking the risk. He'd blocked the comments and ignored every word.

"You weren't ready to hear it." Ever the undercover agent, Connor scanned the parking lot. Watching people as they moved in and out. "So, what was the thing with leaving the hospital room yesterday? You have to know that hurt her."

He hadn't, really. Not until after, when Cam had texted to call him an idiot.

But Shane hadn't been playing games or thinking over his options. He knew he loved her and wanted to be with her, no matter the consequences. But he did have responsibilities and tried to meet them. "I needed to talk with Holt.

I owed him that and wanted to go to Makena with a clear head and no barriers between us."

Connor smiled. "What if Holt had told you to back off?"

It would have ripped him apart, but Shane's answer didn't change. "I would have ignored him."

"Yep, that's love." Connor pushed off from the car and stood up straight. "Okay, good luck."

That sounded ominous. "Luck?"

"It's cute that you don't think you'll need it." Connor shook his head as he waved and kept walking. "I almost feel bad for you."

MAKENA'S BODY BEGGED for sleep. She was ten seconds away from dropping. She'd dozed on and off in that chair. Talked with the team members and her brother. Checked in and managed to get two of Jeff's relatives to stop by.

Helping that guy could be a full-time job, but she didn't plan to let it get away from her like that. She'd been there for him, providing support. He was recovering well and other people he knew, some from whom he'd been estranged for years, were taking over. Now she could rest.

If only she could close her eyes without seeing Shane's face swim in front of her. As she was walking across the parking lot, it happened again. She was wide-awake with her eyes open, yet he seemed to be standing there, right next to her car. She blinked a few times, expecting him to disappear. But no.

If he'd picked this moment to tell her they needed to stay friends, she might just curl up in a ball. A woman could only take so much. Her bruises had bruises. Worse, her heart felt shredded. He'd done that when he walked away. Fine—if he wanted to walk, he should just keep going.

She stopped in front of him but didn't say anything. For a second, neither did he. He leaned against her car and watched her. Stared, really. The intense scrutiny had her squirming.

"What do you want?" It came out harsher than she'd intended, but she didn't have anything left in the tank. She couldn't hide her reactions or control her feelings. She wanted to strike out and scream. Life seemed so unfair at the moment.

"You."

He'd said that once before and she'd bought it. Not this time. "We're not sleeping together again."

He frowned. "I hope that's not true."

"Look, Shane." She inhaled a few times as she worked to keep some portion of the emotional wall she'd built against him in place. "I'm not your consolation prize. I'm not a side benefit to your case."

"No, you're not."

"What are you doing?" The last of her energy drained out of her. Her shoulders slumped and she fought to stay on her feet. "I'm not in the mood for games or for—"

He stepped up and leaned in. Before she could blink, his arms came around her and his lips met hers. He kissed her with a kick of heat and intensity that stole her breath. She held on as his mouth traveled over hers, and her knees buckled.

When he lifted his head again she expected... Actually, she had no idea what to expect. He could have said anything and she would have nodded. Her brain refused to work and every word died in her throat before she could say them.

"I love you."

Her heart jumped. Hope pulsed inside her, but she tamped it down. He was handing her everything, but she feared it meant nothing. She couldn't bring herself to believe, so she shut it all down. "No, you don't."

"You're telling me how I feel?" He sounded amused by the idea.

Nothing about this moment struck her as funny. She shoved against his arms to get him to let go. "Goodbye, Shane."

She fumbled with her keys. They bounced off her fingers and fell to the ground with a clink.

Lost and heartsick, she stood there and tipped her head back to stare up at the sky.

"You can leave, but I'll just follow you." His voice came from right behind her. His hands went to her arms, and his face rested against her hair. "I can't let you go."

He said… She couldn't process the words or anything else that was happening. She turned around to face him, letting him see every ounce of pain running through her. "Is this about your ego?"

"It's about loving you." He rubbed his hands up and down her arms. "About realizing that I was wrong and pushing you away when I should have been grabbing on with all my strength."

That sounded good, but her mind couldn't hold on to a single thought. "I don't understand."

"I'm sorry I let fear and old wounds keep us apart." He balanced his forehead against hers. "I will never do that again."

"You love me?" The words didn't even sound right to her.

He lifted his head and stared down at her. There, written on his face, she saw tenderness and hope, a good bit of lust and, yes, love. She had no idea where or why, but the hope finally took hold. She didn't bat it away or downplay it. She held on.

"Almost losing you nearly killed me." He

lifted her hand and pressed her fingers to his lips. "I don't want to be away from you."

"You were last night." That piece didn't make any sense in light of all the wonderful things he said now.

The corner of Shane's mouth kicked up in a smile. "I had to tell Holt while I didn't need his permission and wasn't asking for it. I hoped we had it."

"I talked with him." She ran through the conversation in her mind. Now some of Holt's stray comments made sense. "He never said anything."

"I asked him to let me win you back first." Shane shrugged. "For the record, he made me work for it."

As if that would be hard. "I bet."

"I would have done and said anything. Though I have to admit you are the one I want to win over, not him."

She tried to imagine that conversation and how hard a time Holt must have given Shane. The idea that he would go through that, that he'd even thought it was important to take on the challenge of winning Holt over, made her smile.

"I love you." She said it because she needed him to know. She'd thrown it out in the heat of the attack. Now, in the middle of the parking lot with people walking by and nothing on the line, she made the vow again. "With all I am and all I have."

"Good."

The response made her laugh. "That's all you've got to say?"

"Definitely not. I have all sorts of things I want to say and do to you. Some of them in bed. Some against a wall. Some on G-rated dates."

She loved the sound of all of it. "You tell me when and where."

"We're going to do this right." He lifted her off the ground and held her tight. "Start over. Not fast-forward the relationship and skip over the good parts."

She wasn't sure she loved that. "Meaning?"

"We're going to date. Go out to eat and do whatever it is dating people do. You'll probably need to help me with that, because I'm clueless."

"You're doing great."

"And, just so you know, I'm going to kiss you…a lot. Like, all the time. In private and sometimes in parking lots, like here." He followed through by doing just that. Planted a kiss filled with promise and love and every great thing on her. It went on and on, and dragged her under.

When he lifted his head again, all the strain around his eyes had disappeared. She couldn't help running her finger over his eyebrows.

"You're going to know every single day how much I love you," he said in a husky voice. "How much you mean to me and how you are my future."

Light burst to life inside her, washing away the exhaustion and the doubts. Her head cleared just as her heart sped up. "We should start now."

He laughed. "Are you making a pass?"

"Do I need to?"

"No, because I'm already yours."

Then she kissed him. Parking lot or no, she wanted her life with him to start right now. "Take me home, so you can make up for leaving me yesterday."

He nodded. "I'm willing to spend a lifetime doing that."

FOUR DAYS LATER Shane still hadn't stopped smiling. He'd survived seeing Holt again. Made it through all the doctor checkups and Makena moving into his place. That last one being the best thing to happen to him in…ever.

Every piece of his life had fallen into place.

He'd been the last bachelor in the group. The only one not attached, and he'd held that as a badge of honor for a long time. Something he now saw as ridiculous.

Maybe he hadn't put a ring on Makena's finger or waited for her at the end of an aisle, but he would. And not years from now—soon. Now that he saw his life with her, he wanted more. There was no reason to wait and see. He knew her. Knew them. Knew that life without her wasn't worth much.

Connor walked into the conference room at team headquarters and dropped a file in front of Shane. "You ready to get back to work?"

He glanced around. "Am I the only one on this case?"

"Nah, that's your expense voucher."

Shane opened the file and stared at the pages. He had a check coming his way. Yeah, so what? It didn't mean much to him. "Okay."

Connor leaned back in his chair at the head of the table and grabbed a thick stack of folders off the long desk in front of the line of monitors. "I actually wanted you to look through these."

The pile landed on the table with a thud. Shane had no idea what he was looking at or why. He could scan every page or he could just ask. "What's going on?"

"Potential candidates."

"For?" Shane opened the cover of the top one and glanced inside.

"To be Corcoran Team members." Connor folded his arms in front of him and leaned against the table. "It's time."

They'd been so insular for so long. Connor

rarely added new people. He talked about the need for camaraderie and joked that with too many members he risked being overruled. As if that would ever happen. He had their loyalty and trust, and they were not men who gave either easily.

Just so he was clear, he tried again. "We're hiring?"

"I'm thinking we need a West Coast office." Connor shrugged. "That will allow all of you room to pick and choose cases and spend some more time closer to home."

That didn't sound like the tough sharpshooter Shane knew. Sure, Connor had been married to Jana for years and spent his days protecting others and loving her. But making sure the rest of them had stable home lives? Interesting.

"Are you matchmaking?" Shane couldn't even make the idea make sense in his head.

"Blame my wife."

That, Shane got. Something about keeping Makena happy appealed to him. He hated when she so much as frowned. Shane didn't mind the travel or the work. Still, the idea of spending most nights by her side in their big bed didn't exactly stink.

Thank you, Jana. "I love your wife."

Connor did what he always did. Spun his

wedding ring around on his finger without even realizing he did it. "You are not alone."

"It won't be easy to find qualified men and women who fit in around here." Shane tried to imagine interviewing people and putting them through a series of tests. A daunting but interesting task.

"It takes a certain kind of crazy, I agree."

No question about that. "Do you have people in mind?"

Shane could think of a few. There were folks he'd worked with over the years whom he could see stepping up and assuming the kinds of risks they took for granted. Strong and decent people who needed to find a purpose, which was exactly what he had been. Lost and wandering. Now he had the best friends of his life, a woman he loved and a team that meant everything to him.

Connor nodded in the direction of the high stack. "Right there. I want you all to take a look and offer feedback. Take your time. There's no rush. This is about finding the right people, not speed."

And that summed up why Connor was in charge. Why he inspired so much loyalty. "Sounds good to me."

"Besides that, we need a few bachelors around here." Connor leaned back in his chair. "I thought you'd never go down. And so easy? Man, you're lucky."

He'd never thought so before, but Shane sure thought so now. "Easy?"

"She should have made you beg."

Shane couldn't help smiling. "She does… sometimes."

Connor leaned forward and the legs of his chair hit the floor. "That's probably too much information."

"I'm happy."

"And I'm happy for you." Connor got up and walked around the table. "Now get ready so you can get home to Makena."

Shane would never tire of hearing that. "You got it, boss."

* * * * *

Read on for a sneak peek of
LONE RIDER
The next installment in
THE MONTANA HAMILTONS *series*
from New York Times *bestselling author*
B.J. Daniels.
When danger claims her, rescue comes from
the one man she least expects...

CHAPTER ONE

THE MOMENT JACE CALDER saw his sister's face, he feared the worst. His heart sank. Emily, his troubled little sister, had been doing so well since she'd gotten the job at the Sarah Hamilton Foundation in Big Timber, Montana.

"What's wrong?" he asked as he removed his Stetson, pulled up a chair at the Big Timber Java coffee shop and sat down across from her. Tossing his hat on the seat of an adjacent chair, he braced himself for bad news.

Emily blinked her big blue eyes. Even though she was closing in on twenty-five, he often caught glimpses of the girl she'd been. Her pixie cut, once a dark brown like his own hair, was dyed black. From thirteen on, she'd been piercing anything she could. At sixteen she'd begun getting tattoos and drinking. It wasn't until she'd turned seventeen that she'd run away, taken up with a thirty-year-old biker drug-dealer thief and ended up in jail for the first time.

But while Emily still had the tattoos and the piercings, she'd changed after the birth of her daughter, and after snagging this job with Bo Hamilton.

"What's wrong is Bo," his sister said. Bo had insisted her employees at the foundation call her by her first name. "Pretty cool for a boss, huh?" his sister had said at the time. He'd been surprised. That didn't sound like the woman he knew.

But who knew what was in Bo's head lately. Four months ago her mother, Sarah, who everyone believed dead the past twenty-two years, had suddenly shown up out of nowhere. According to what he'd read in the papers, Sarah had no memory of the past twenty-two years.

He'd been worried it would hurt the foundation named for her. Not to mention what a shock it must have been for Bo.

Emily leaned toward him and whispered, "Bo's... She's gone."

"Gone?"

"Before she left Friday, she told me that she would be back by ten this morning. She hasn't shown up, and no one knows where she is."

That *did* sound like the Bo Hamilton he knew. The thought of her kicked up that old ache inside him. He'd been glad when Emily had found a job and moved back to town with her baby girl. But he'd often wished her employer had been anyone but Bo Hamilton—the woman he'd once asked to marry him.

He'd spent the past five years avoiding Bo, which wasn't easy in a county as small as Sweet Grass. Crossing paths with her, even after five years, still hurt. It riled him in a way that only made him mad at himself for letting her get to him after all this time.

"What do you mean, *gone?*" he asked now.

Emily looked pained. "I probably shouldn't be telling you this—"

"Em," he said impatiently. She'd been doing so well at this job, and she'd really turned her life around. He couldn't bear the thought that Bo's disappearance might derail her second chance. Em's three-year-old daughter, Jodie, desperately needed her mom to stay on track.

Leaning closer again, she whispered, "Apparently there are funds missing from the foundation. An auditor's been going over all the records since Friday."

He sat back in surprise. No matter what he thought of Bo, he'd never imagined this. The woman was already rich. She wouldn't need to divert funds...

"And that's not the worst of it," Emily said. "I was told she's on a camping trip in the mountains."

"So, she isn't really gone."

Em waved a hand. "She took her camping gear, saddled up and left Saturday afternoon. Apparently she's the one who called the auditor, so she knew he would be finished and wanting to talk to her this morning!"

Jace considered this news. If Bo really were on the run with the money, wouldn't she take her passport and her SUV as far as the nearest airport? But why would she run at all? He doubted Bo had ever had a problem that her daddy, the senator, hadn't fixed for her. She'd always had a safety net. Unlike him.

He'd been on his own since eighteen. He'd been a senior in high school, struggling to pay the bills, hang on to the ranch and raise his wild kid sister after his parents had been killed in a small plane crash. He'd managed to save the ranch, but he hadn't been equipped to raise Emily and had made his share of mistakes.

A few months ago, his sister had got out of jail and gone to work for Bo. He'd been surprised she'd given Emily a chance. He'd had to readjust his opinion of Bo—but only a little. Now this.

"There has to be an explanation," he said, even though he knew firsthand that Bo often acted impulsively. She did whatever she wanted, damn the world. But now his little sister was part of that world. How could she leave Emily and the rest of the staff at the foundation to face this alone?

"I sure hope everything is all right," his sister said. "Bo is so sweet."

Sweet wasn't a word he would have used to describe her. Sexy in a cowgirl way, yes, since most of the time she dressed in jeans, boots and a Western shirt—all of which accented her very nice curves. Her long, sandy-blond hair was often pulled up in a ponytail or wrestled into a braid that hung over one shoulder. Since her wide green eyes didn't need makeup to give her that girl-next-door look, she seldom wore it.

"I can't believe she wouldn't show up. Something must have happened," Emily said loyally.

He couldn't help being skeptical based on Bo's history. But given Em's concern, he didn't want to add his own kindling to the fire.

"Jace, I just have this bad feeling. You're the best tracker in these parts. I know it's a lot to ask, but would you go find her?"

He almost laughed. Given the bad blood between him and Bo? "I'm the last person—"

"I'm really worried about her. I know she wouldn't run off."

Jace wished *he* knew that. "Look, if you're really that concerned, maybe you should call the sheriff. He can get search and rescue—"

"No," Emily cried. "No one knows what's

going on over at the foundation. We have to keep this quiet. That's why you have to go."

He'd never been able to deny his little sister anything, but this was asking too much.

"Please, Jace."

He swore silently. Maybe he'd get lucky and Bo would return before he even got saddled up. "If you're that worried…" He got to his feet and reached for his hat, telling himself it shouldn't take him long to find Bo if she'd gone up into the Crazies, as the Crazy Mountains were known locally. He'd grown up in those mountains. His father had been an avid hunter who'd taught him everything about mountain survival.

If Bo had gone rogue with the foundation's funds… He hated to think what that would do not only to Emily's job but also to her recovery. She idolized her boss. So did Josie, who was allowed the run of the foundation office.

But finding Bo was one thing. Bringing her back to face the music might be another. He started to say as much to Emily, but she cut him off.

"Oh, Jace, thank you so much. If anyone can find her, it's you."

He smiled at his sister as he set his Stetson firmly on his head and made her a promise. "I'll find Bo Hamilton and bring her back." One way or the other.

CHAPTER TWO

BO HAMILTON ROSE with the sun, packed up camp and saddled up as a squirrel chattered at her from a nearby pine tree. Overhead, high in the Crazy Mountains, Montana's big, cloudless early summer sky had turned a brilliant blue. The day was already warm. Before she'd left, she'd heard a storm was coming in, but she'd known she'd be out of the mountains long before it hit.

She'd had a devil of a time getting to sleep last night, and after tossing and turning for hours in her sleeping bag, she had finally fallen into a death-like sleep.

But this morning, she'd awakened ready to face whatever would be awaiting her tomorrow back at the office in town. Coming up here in the mountains had been the best thing she could have done. For months she'd been worried and confused as small amounts of money kept disappearing from the foundation.

Then last week, she'd realized that more than

a hundred thousand dollars was gone. She'd been so shocked that she hadn't been able to breathe, let alone think. That's when she'd called in an independent auditor. She just hoped she could find out what had happened to the money before anyone got wind of it—especially her father, Senator Buckmaster Hamilton.

Her stomach roiled at the thought. He'd always been so proud of her for taking over the reins of the foundation that bore her mother's name. All her father needed was another scandal. He was running for the presidency of the United States, something he'd dreamed of for years. Now his daughter was about to go to jail for embezzlement. She could only imagine his disappointment in her—not to mention what it might do to the foundation.

She loved the work the foundation did, helping small businesses in their community. Her father had been worried that she couldn't handle the responsibility. She'd been determined to show him he was wrong. And show herself, as well. She'd grown up a lot in the past five years, and running the foundation had given her a sense of purpose she'd badly needed.

That's why she was anxious to find out the results of the audit now that her head was clear. The mountains always did that for her. Breathing in the fresh air now, she swung up in the saddle, spurred her horse and headed down the trail toward the ranch. She'd camped only a couple of hours back into the mountain, so she still had plenty of time, she thought as she rode. The last thing she wanted was to be late to meet with the auditor.

She'd known for some time that there were... *discrepancies* in foundation funds. A part of her had hoped that it was merely a mistake—that someone would realize he or she had made an error—so she wouldn't have to confront anyone about the slip.

Bo knew how naive that was, but she couldn't bear to think that one of her employees was behind the theft. Yes, her employees were a ragtag bunch. There was Albert Drum, a seventy-two-year-young former banker who worked with the recipients of the foundation loans. Emily Calder, twenty-four, took care of the website, research, communication and marketing. The only other employee was forty-eight-year-old widow Norma Branstetter, who was in charge of fund-raising.

Employees and board members reviewed the applications that came in for financial help. But Bo was the one responsible for the money that came and went through the foundation.

Unfortunately, she trusted her employees so much that she often let them run the place, including dealing with the financial end of things. She hadn't been paying close enough attention. How else could there be unexplained expenditures?

Her father had warned her about the people she hired, saying she had to be careful. But she loved giving jobs to those who desperately needed another chance. Her employees had become a second family to her.

Just the thought that one of her employees might be responsible made her sick to her stomach. True, she was a sucker for a hard-luck story. But she trusted the people she'd hired. The thought brought tears to her eyes. They all tried so hard and were so appreciative of their jobs. She refused to believe any one of them would steal from the foundation.

So what had happened to the missing funds?

She hadn't ridden far when her horse nickered and raised his head as if sniffing the wind. Spurring him forward, she continued through the dense trees. The pine boughs sighed in the breeze, releasing the smells of early summer in the mountains she'd grown up with. She loved the Crazy Mountains. She loved them especially at this time of year. They rose from the valley into high snow-capped peaks, the awe-inspiring range running for miles to the north like a mountainous island in a sea of grassy plains.

What she appreciated most about the Crazies was that a person could get lost in them, she thought. A hunter had done just that last year.

She'd ridden down the ridge some distance, the sun moving across the sky over her head, before she caught the strong smell of smoke. This morning she'd put her campfire out using the creek water nearby. Too much of Montana burned every summer because of lightning storms and careless people, so she'd made sure her fire was extinguished before she'd left.

Now reining in, she spotted the source of the smoke. A small campfire burned below her in the dense trees of a protected gully. She stared down into the camp as smoke curled up. While it wasn't that unusual to stumble across a backpacker this deep in the Crazies, it *was* strange for a camp to be so far off the trail. Also, she didn't see anyone below her on the mountain near the fire. Had whoever camped there failed to put out the fire before leaving?

Bo hesitated, feeling torn because she didn't want to take the time to ride all the way down the mountain to the out-of-the-way camp. Nor did she want to ride into anyone's camp unless necessary.

But if the camper had failed to put out the fire, that was another story.

"Hello?" she called down the mountainside.

A hawk let out a cry overhead, momentarily startling her.

"Hello?" she called again, louder.

No answer. No sign of anyone in the camp.

Bo let out an aggravated sigh and spurred her horse. She had a long ride back and didn't need a detour. But she still had plenty of time if she hurried. As she made her way down into the ravine, she caught glimpses of the camp and the smoking campfire, but nothing else.

The hidden-away camp finally came into view below her. She could see that whoever had camped there hadn't made any effort at all to put out the fire. She looked for horseshoe tracks but saw only boot prints in the dust that led down to the camp.

A quiet seemed to fall over the mountainside. No hawk called out again from high above the trees. No squirrel chattered at her from a pine bough. Even the breeze seemed to have gone silent.

Bo felt a sudden chill as if the sun had gone down—an instant before the man appeared so suddenly from out of the dense darkness of the trees. He grabbed her, yanked her down from the saddle and clamped an arm around her as he shoved the dirty blade of a knife in her face.

"Well, look at you," he said hoarsely against

her ear. "Ain't you a sight for sore eyes? Guess it's my lucky day."

JACE HAD JUST knocked at the door when another truck drove up from the direction of the corrals. As Senator Buckmaster Hamilton himself opened the door, he looked past Jace's shoulder. Jace glanced back to see Cooper Barnett climb out of his truck and walk toward them.

Jace turned back around. "I'm Jace Calder," he said, holding out his hand as the senator's gaze shifted to him.

The senator frowned but shook his hand. "I know who you are. I'm just wondering what's got you on my doorstep so early in the morning."

"I'm here about your daughter Bo."

Buckmaster looked to Cooper. "Tell me you aren't here about my daughter Olivia."

Cooper laughed. "My pregnant bride is just fine, thanks."

The senator let out an exaggerated breath and turned his attention back to Jace. "What's this about—" But before he could finish, a tall, elegant blonde woman appeared at his side. Jace recognized Angelina Broadwater Hamilton, the senator's second wife. The rumors about her being kicked out of the house to make way for Buckmaster's first wife weren't true, it seemed.

She put a hand on Buckmaster's arm. "It's the

auditor calling from the foundation office. He's looking for Bo. She didn't show up for work today, and there seems to be a problem."

"That's why I'm here," Jace said.

"Me, too," Cooper said, sounding surprised.

"Come in, then," Buckmaster said, waving both men inside. Once he'd closed the big door behind them, he asked, "Now, what's this about Bo?"

"I was just talking to one of the wranglers," Cooper said, jumping in ahead of Jace. "Bo apparently left Saturday afternoon on horseback, saying she'd be back this morning, but she hasn't returned."

"That's what I heard, as well," Jace said, taking the opening. "I need to know where she might have gone."

Both Buckmaster and Cooper looked to him. "You sound as if you're planning to go after her," the senator said.

"I am."

"Why would you do that? I didn't think you two were seeing each other?" Cooper asked like the protective brother-in-law he was.

"We're not," Jace said.

"Wait a minute," the senator said. "You're the one who stood her up for the senior prom. I'll never forget it. My baby cried for weeks."

Jace nodded. "That would be me."

"But you've dated Bo more recently than senior prom," Buckmaster was saying.

"Five years ago," he said. "But that doesn't have anything to do with this. I have my reasons for wanting to see Bo come back. My sister works at the foundation."

"Why wouldn't Bo come back?" the senator demanded.

Behind him, Angelina made a disparaging sound. "Because there's money missing from the foundation along with your daughter." She looked at Jace. "You said your sister works down there?"

He smiled, seeing that she was clearly judgmental of the "kind of people" Bo had hired to work at the foundation. "My sister doesn't have access to any of the money, if that's what you're worried about." He turned to the senator again. "The auditor is down at the foundation office, trying to sort it out. Bo needs to be there. I thought you might have some idea where she might have gone in the mountains. I thought I'd go find her."

The senator looked to his son-in-law. Cooper shrugged.

"Cooper, you were told she planned to be back Sunday?" her father said. "She probably changed her mind or went too far, not realizing how long it would take her to get back. If she had an appointment today with an auditor, I'm sure she's on her way as we speak."

"Or she's hiding up there and doesn't want to be found," Angelina quipped from the couch. "If she took that money, she could be miles from here by now." She groaned. "It's always something with your girls, isn't it?"

"I highly doubt Bo has taken off with any foundation money," the senator said and shot his wife a disgruntled look. "Every minor problem isn't a major scandal," he said and sighed, clearly irritated with his wife.

When he and Bo had dated, she'd told him that her stepmother was always quick to blame her and her sisters no matter the situation. As far as Jace could tell, there was no love lost on either side.

"Maybe we should call the sheriff," Cooper said.

Angelina let out a cry. "That's all we need—more negative publicity. It will be bad enough when this gets out. But if search and rescue is called in and the sheriff has to go up there… For all we know, Bo could be meeting someone in those mountains."

Jace hadn't considered she might have an accomplice. "That's why I'm the best person to go after her."

"How do you figure that?" Cooper demanded, giving him a hard look.

"She already doesn't like me, and the feeling is mutual. Maybe you're right and she's hightailing it home as we speak," Jace said. "But whatever's going on with her, I'm going to find her and make sure she gets back."

"You sound pretty confident of that," the senator said sounding almost amused.

"I know these mountains, and I'm not a bad tracker. I'll find her. But that's big country. My search would go faster if I have some idea where she was headed when she left."

"There's a trail to the west of the ranch that connects with the Sweet Grass Creek trail," her father said.

Jace rubbed a hand over his jaw. "That trail forks not far up."

"She usually goes to the first camping spot before the fork," the senator said. "It's only a couple of hours back in. I'm sure she wouldn't go any farther than that. It's along Loco Creek."

"I know that spot," Jace said.

Cooper looked to his father-in-law. "You want me to get some men together and go search for her? That makes more sense than sending—"

Buckmaster shook his head and turned to Jace. "I remember your father. The two of you were volunteers on a search years ago. I was impressed with both of you. I'm putting my money on you finding her if she doesn't turn up on her own. I'll give you 'til sundown."

"Make it twenty-four hours. There's a storm coming so I plan to be back before it hits. If we're both not back by then, send in the cavalry," he said and with a tip of his hat, headed for the door.

Behind him, he heard Cooper say, "Sending him could be a mistake."

"The cowboy's mistake," Buckmaster said. "I know my daughter. She's on her way back, and she isn't going to like that young man tracking her down. Jace Calder is the one she almost married."

Find out what happens next in
LONE RIDER
by New York Times
bestselling author B.J. Daniels
available August 2015,
wherever HQN Books and ebooks are sold.
www.Harlequin.com